THE CEO OF THE MIND

SWAPNIL KHAMKAR

To my parents, whose love and values have shaped who I am.
To the timeless teachings of Swami Vivekananda, which continue to illuminate the path for countless souls.
And to every seeker on the journey of self-discovery, may you find the light within.

Contents

Contents

Foreword

The modern world often measures success by external markers: wealth, fame, and achievements. Yet, beneath these pursuits lies an undeniable truth — true fulfillment comes from mastering the mind and uncovering the deeper purpose of life.

This book, *The CEO of the Mind*, is more than just a story. It is a mirror for our own struggles, aspirations, and journeys. Through Leo's transformation, readers will find echoes of their own potential to transcend challenges and embrace inner peace.

Drawing inspiration from the profound teachings of Swami Vivekananda, this book presents timeless wisdom in an engaging narrative format, making ancient principles accessible and relatable to modern readers.

It is a privilege to introduce this work by Swapnil Khamkar, a visionary leader and author dedicated to spreading the essence of mindfulness and empowerment. I believe this book will inspire, uplift, and guide readers toward a more meaningful life.

Sanjay Khamkar

Preface

The idea for *The CEO of the Mind* was born from my reflections on the challenges of modern life. In a world that often glorifies material success, we risk losing touch with the true purpose of our existence.

Through Leo Harper's journey, I sought to blend storytelling with timeless teachings to create a narrative that inspires personal transformation. Each chapter is a step in Leo's awakening, reflecting lessons that resonate deeply with all of us.

This book is not just a story but an invitation — an invitation to pause, reflect, and reconnect with the wisdom that resides within each of us. It draws heavily from the teachings of Swami Vivekananda, whose insights into the human mind and spirit remain profoundly relevant today.

I hope this book serves as a guide, a companion, and a source of inspiration for anyone seeking to master their mind and live with purpose.

With gratitude,
Swapnil Khamkar

Acknowledgements

This book would not have been possible without the love, guidance, and support of so many incredible individuals who have been a part of my journey.

First and foremost, I express my deepest gratitude to my parents, Sanjay Khamkar and Pratibha Khamkar, for their unconditional love and for instilling in me the values that guide my life. To my beloved wife, Yashasvi Khamkar, thank you for being my partner in every sense; your unwavering support means the world to me.

To Pushpak Khamkar and Vrushali Khamkar, your encouragement has been a pillar of strength. I also honor the blessings of my grandparents, Harishchandra Khamkar and Taramati Khamkar, whose love and wisdom have shaped me profoundly.

I extend heartfelt thanks to my mentors, Prof. Dr. Vasant Desale sir and Prof. Ganpat Shelke sir, whose guidance and insights have inspired me to achieve more than I thought possible.

I owe a deep sense of gratitude to the timeless teachings of Swami Vivekananda, whose wisdom and vision continue to inspire and guide me every single day. His philosophy has profoundly influenced my personal journey and the vision of this book.

Lastly, to my readers: thank you for choosing this book and for being a part of this journey. Your willingness to explore new perspectives and embark on a path of transformation gives meaning to this work.

With profound gratitude,
Swapnil Khamkar

CHAPTER ONE

Leo Harper's office was a gleaming shrine to ambition. On the thirty-seventh floor of one of New York's tallest buildings, his corner office offered sweeping views of the city below, its streets alive with the energy of millions, yet all of it felt like a distant hum to him. The office itself was a reflection of his empire—polished, sleek, minimalist—each piece of furniture carefully selected to convey power, sophistication, and control. The walls were adorned with abstract art that seemed to tell a story of success, but for Leo, it was a story that had begun to ring hollow.

Today, his eyes rested on the latest deal sprawled across his desk: an aggressive entry into the smartphone market. It was a surefire move, one that would expand his company's reach and cement Harper Technologies as a tech juggernaut. His team had run the numbers over and over, each calculation promising exponential growth. The strategy was flawless, the potential clear. And yet, as Leo stared at the proposal, a strange feeling washed over him—one he could no longer ignore.

Success. The word echoed in his mind like a hollow drumbeat.

It had been the goal, the singular focus for the last twenty years. He had built Harper Technologies from nothing—sacrificing friendships, relationships, and more than he cared to admit. And yet, now that he had it all—money, power, influence—he felt a gnawing emptiness inside, a hollow space that no amount of achievement seemed able to fill. The thrill of victory had dulled, leaving behind only the quiet hum of a machine that kept moving, even when the person inside it had stopped feeling anything.

His phone buzzed, pulling him from his thoughts. It was a text from Claire. *"Are we still on for dinner tonight?"*

Leo's finger hovered over the screen, the question lingering. Dinner. A routine they had maintained, like so many others. A dinner where they'd eat, discuss their days, but never really *talk*. Not about what really mattered. Not about the distance that had grown between them. Not about the emptiness he couldn't seem to shake.

He exhaled slowly and typed back a quick reply. *"Yes, of course, I'll be there."*

The words felt automatic, and with a sense of resignation, he put his phone down. Dinner. It was always the same—two people sitting across from each other, sharing a meal, but sharing little else. Their conversations had become a routine, and the silence between them had become more deafening than any words.

Leo looked back at the deal on his desk. The smartphone market. It was a game-changer. Yet, even as his mind acknowledged its potential, his heart remained unmoved. *Was this really it?* he wondered. The culmination of a life spent chasing success? A life spent climbing higher and higher, only to realize that the summit was as empty as the base from which he had started?

The city stretched before him, alive with its frenetic energy, but Leo felt detached, like an observer rather than a participant. His eyes traced the lines of the streets below, the endless grid of concrete and glass, and yet none of it seemed to reach him. The millions of lives out there, each one chasing their own dreams, seemed like distant echoes, like the passing of time that no longer mattered.

A knock on the door jolted him from his reverie.

"Mr. Harper?" It was Sarah, his assistant. She was standing in the doorway, her expression unreadable. "The board meeting is about to start. Are you ready?"

Leo glanced at the clock. Another meeting, another presentation, another set of numbers and projections. The world he had created, the world he had fought so hard to build, was waiting for him. But in that moment, it felt like a weight he could no longer bear.

"Yes, let's begin," he said, forcing a smile. He stood, smoothing the cuffs of his suit and taking a deep breath. His reflection in the glass felt like that of a stranger—someone who had everything and yet, in some profound way, nothing at all.

As he stepped into the boardroom, the faces of his executives greeted him with smiles, but Leo could feel their eyes on him, searching for that familiar spark, that unmistakable drive that had once burned so fiercely within him. But it was missing now. Gone, like the last ember in a dying fire.

"Leo, great to have you here," Jack, his COO, greeted him. He was mid-sentence, already diving into the details of the upcoming venture. "We've crunched the numbers, and the opportunity in the smartphone market is huge. With your leadership, we'll be able to corner the market in just a few years."

Leo nodded absently, taking his seat at the head of the table. The meeting droned on. Projections, strategies, financial breakdowns—all the things that were supposed to excite him. But instead, he felt detached, as if he were listening to someone else's dream.

At some point, Jack asked, "Leo, any thoughts?"

Leo blinked, realizing that they were all waiting for him. "It looks solid," he replied, his voice mechanical. "Let's move forward."

The words felt like they were coming from someone else's mouth, but he couldn't seem to stop them.

The meeting continued, but Leo's mind had already wandered. He could feel his pulse slow, the weight of the room pressing in on him. *Why does it all feel so... empty?* he wondered. The deals, the decisions, the endless cycle of expansion—none of it seemed to hold any real meaning anymore.

Finally, the meeting came to a close. His team filed out, leaving Leo alone in the spacious room, the echo of their departure hanging in the air like the fading sound of a bell. He sat back in his chair, hands pressed to his temples, trying to make sense of the ache that had settled deep inside him.

"Mr. Harper?"

Leo looked up to see Sarah standing in the doorway again. She had a hesitant look on her face. "Is everything alright?" she asked softly. "You've seemed... off today."

Leo forced a smile, but it didn't reach his eyes. "Just tired," he said, his voice thin. "I'll be fine. Thanks, Sarah."

She nodded and left him in solitude once more.

Leo stared at the empty chair across from him. *Claire.* She was still waiting for him. Would dinner be another night of hollow conversation? Another night of pretending that everything was fine, when he knew deep down that it wasn't?

His phone buzzed once more, pulling him from his thoughts. It was Claire again. Her message read, *"I need to talk. Something's wrong, Leo."*

The words hit him like a punch to the gut. Claire had always been his anchor, but lately, even she seemed to be slipping through his fingers.

Dinner. It wasn't just dinner. It was a lifeline, a last attempt to reconnect with the woman he had once loved so deeply. He typed a response, his fingers trembling as he did. *"I'm on my way."*

He stood up, buttoning his jacket. As he walked out of his office, the weight of the decision he had just made lingered in the air. The world outside buzzed with life, but Leo was no longer part of it. He had climbed so high, but now, for the first time, he found himself questioning what he had built. What it all meant.

He stepped into the elevator, the doors sliding closed with a soft *ding.* He looked at his reflection in the polished metal.

Who was this man?

For the first time in years, Leo Harper didn't have an answer.

As the elevator descended, so too did the walls he had built around himself. A feeling, deep and unsettling, began to settle in his chest. The illusion of success had shattered, and Leo was left to face the truth.

CHAPTER TWO

Leo Harper was used to the hum of the city, the perpetual motion of a world that never paused for anything or anyone. But as he walked through the front door of his sleek Manhattan apartment, the silence that greeted him felt as suffocating as the constant noise outside. The weight of the day's meetings, deals, and decisions hung over him like a cloud, but it was the absence of sound in his home that hit him hardest.

Claire's message from earlier echoed in his mind— *"I need to talk. Something's wrong, Leo."* He had ignored it, convincing himself that dinner would somehow patch the cracks in their relationship. But as he stood at the threshold, the cool air of the apartment sweeping over him, he felt the first tremors of doubt. He had always been the man who could fix things, who could make decisions that would steer his company into success. But this? This was different.

The living room, with its muted colors and modern furniture, looked immaculate—too immaculate. The kind of pristine that only existed when no one had touched anything in days. Leo moved silently through the room, his steps echoing on the polished hardwood floors. Claire wasn't here. She had stopped waiting up for him, stopped pretending that everything was fine. She had done it with such grace, Leo couldn't even fault her for it. She had once been his anchor, the calm in his storm, but somewhere along the way, that anchor had slipped from his grasp.

As he entered the kitchen, he found a note on the counter, folded neatly. It was from Claire.

"Leo, I can't keep doing this. I'm not sure what I'm still holding onto. We need to talk, but I don't know if anything will change. You've chosen this life, and I've been a part of it, but not really with you. I need more than this. More than your promises. More than this endless chase. I hope you realize that soon."

The words hit him like a slap in the face. He closed his eyes, leaning against the counter, the weight of her absence pressing into him. What had he done? How had it come to this? He had been so focused on building the empire, on scaling new heights, that he had forgotten about the one thing that had once mattered most—his family.

But it wasn't just Claire. His mother's voice was also a constant in the back of his mind, bitter and unrelenting, like a refrain he couldn't escape. He had promised her that the family business, the one that had been in the Harper name for generations, would stay in their hometown, in the heart of Pennsylvania. But when he had moved the company to New York, chasing the promise of bigger opportunities and higher profits, she had been devastated.

"You've abandoned your roots, Leo," she had told him when he had finally broken the news over the phone. "You've turned your back on everything your father built, everything we've worked for."

He had dismissed her words then, as he always had. But now, in the quiet of his apartment, the guilt gnawed at him. She wasn't wrong. The family business had been his father's legacy, and moving it to the fast-paced streets of Manhattan had been a betrayal in her eyes. The last time they spoke, his mother's voice had cracked with disappointment.

"Don't come back here expecting anything from me, Leo," she had said. "You've made your choices. You've chosen your empire over family. I can't pretend to support that."

His father had passed away before Leo ever had a chance to prove to him that he could be the man who would carry on the business and grow it. But his mother? She had always been his unwavering supporter. Now, she felt like a shadow, a distant echo of the woman who had once believed in his potential, before he had become consumed by his own ambition.

The sound of the door opening startled him. Claire's silhouette appeared in the doorway, her tired eyes meeting his. She was home. But she wasn't alone—she hadn't been for a while.

"Claire," Leo said, his voice tight. "I—"

"You're here," she said, cutting him off. "Finally. Where have you been? Again."

She wasn't angry, not in the way he had expected. There was no shouting, no accusations. Just the soft resignation in her voice that made it even harder to bear. She wasn't asking for an explanation. She had stopped doing that a long time ago.

"I've been busy," Leo replied, almost apologetically. The words felt weak, inadequate. He could already feel the familiar wall between them rising again, this time taller and thicker than before.

"Too busy to notice your own life falling apart?" Claire's words were soft but cutting. She wasn't trying to wound him, but somehow, it stung deeper than any confrontation ever could. "Leo, you've chosen this life, this constant chase. You've chosen it over me, over us."

Leo ran a hand through his hair, the weight of her words settling heavily on his chest. This wasn't how he had envisioned his life turning out. He had always thought that the success would bring happiness, that the more he built, the more everything else would fall into place. But now, in the quiet of their apartment, with Claire standing in front of him, the truth was undeniable.

"Claire, I—" he started, but the words faltered. He didn't know how to fix it anymore. He had spent so many years building a future that he hadn't stopped to consider what kind of future it would be. He had all the power in the world, but none of it mattered if it didn't have anyone to share it with.

"Leo, I don't want your money," Claire said quietly, her voice almost a whisper. "I don't want your status or your empire. I just want you. The man you used to be. The man who would look at me and smile, not the man who's always looking past me to the next deal. I don't know who you are anymore."

Leo opened his mouth to respond, but the words wouldn't come. He had spent so long convincing himself that success was everything that he had forgotten about the people who truly mattered. His mother, Claire—how had he let them slip away?

"Your mom called again today," Claire continued, her voice tinged with sadness. "She said you haven't even visited her in months. She misses you, Leo."

Leo's heart sank at the mention of his mother. His relationship with her had always been complicated, but it had been something he could count on. But now, even she had grown distant, hurt by the choices he had made.

"I'm sorry," Leo muttered, feeling the weight of the apology suffocating him. "I've been so caught up in everything. I didn't mean to—"

"I know you didn't mean to, Leo," Claire interrupted, her voice breaking. "But intentions don't fix things. Actions do. And right now, you're choosing your empire over the people who love you. It's not enough anymore. It never was."

For a moment, they stood there in silence, the distance between them more palpable than the words they hadn't said. Claire's eyes held a sorrow that Leo couldn't seem to undo, a sadness that felt like it had been building for years.

"You can't keep running, Leo," Claire said softly. "You've been running for so long, and now you're losing everything in the process. It's time to stop."

Leo felt his heart clench at her words, but he didn't know how to stop. The chase, the deals, the power—it was all he had known for so long. He had built it all, and it had defined him. But now, with Claire's words hanging in the air, he began to wonder whether it had all been worth it.

In that moment, Leo Harper realized that the empire he had spent his life building was crumbling—right before his eyes. And no amount of success could fix the fractures that ran deep within his family.

CHAPTER THREE

The meeting room buzzed with a hum of excitement, a quiet anticipation that hovered in the air as Leo Harper sat at the head of the table. Before him lay the blueprint for a decision that could reshape the future of Harper Technologies—an ambitious merger with one of the largest tech giants in the world. The figures on the screen were staggering. Billions of dollars, market dominance, and a promise of unmatched growth. The kind of success Leo had been chasing for years.

"This is it, Leo," Jack, his COO, said, his voice filled with a mix of enthusiasm and reverence. "This deal will not only secure Harper Technology's place at the top, it will make us untouchable. The financials are sound. We've done the projections. We're looking at a potential 40% increase in profits within the first year alone."

Leo leaned back in his chair, studying the numbers that danced on the screen in front of him. His mind was already racing, envisioning the boardrooms he would dominate, the accolades that would follow, the financial rewards that would solidify his legacy. Everything was aligned perfectly. The deal was as good as sealed, but as his eyes scanned the room, he couldn't ignore the flicker of unease that lingered at the back of his mind.

"Everything looks great," Leo said, his voice steady, betraying none of the internal conflict that churned within him. "But what's the catch? There's always a catch."

Jack's smile faltered. "Well, there is the matter of job cuts. Merging with them will mean streamlining operations. The company's workforce will need to be reduced significantly. But honestly, Leo, in the long run, it's a necessary step to ensure we remain competitive."

Leo nodded slowly. He had known this part was coming. The layoffs. The fallout. It was a sacrifice he had reconciled with years ago. He had always justified the casualties of progress—those whose lives would be upended by the decisions he made in the pursuit of greatness. After all, businesses grow. The world moves forward. And those who couldn't keep up... well, they fell behind.

But for a moment, Leo's thoughts wandered back to the thousands of people who had poured their hearts into Harper Technologies. The employees who had been with him since the beginning. He had built this company not just with innovation, but with people—real people who had trusted him, followed him, and believed in the dream he had sold them. What would happen to them once the deal was signed?

"Let's move forward," Leo finally said, snapping himself back to reality. "We'll make the announcement next week. The merger is happening."

The room erupted in murmurs of approval. Everyone seemed to see the deal as a win, a victory in the making. But as Leo stood up to leave, a quiet voice echoed in his mind. Was it really a victory if it came at the cost of so many livelihoods?

That evening, Leo returned to his apartment, the weight of the decision pressing down on him more than he had anticipated. The glass walls of the high-rise offered a panoramic view of the city, but tonight, the lights seemed distant—almost mocking, as if they belonged to another world entirely.

As he walked through the door, Claire was already sitting at the kitchen table, a mug of tea in front of her. Her eyes lifted as he entered, and for the first time in what felt like forever, Leo saw the fatigue in them. The weariness that had taken root in their marriage, that had crept in quietly but now stood before them, undeniable.

"You look like you've made up your mind," Claire said, her voice measured but tinged with something darker. "About the merger, I mean."

Leo hesitated, his hand on the doorknob, unsure of how to respond. The room felt too small, too confined for the enormity of what he had just decided.

"I have," he said, finally turning to face her. "It's the right move, Claire. It will secure the future of the company. It will take us to the next level."

Claire's eyes narrowed, her lips pressing into a thin line. She stood up, her chair scraping against the floor with a sound that seemed to reverberate through the room. "The next level?" she repeated, her voice rising slightly. "The next level of what, Leo? The next level of greed? Of soulless ambition?"

Leo's stomach twisted at her words. It wasn't the first time Claire had questioned his decisions, but tonight, the dissonance between them felt sharper, more pointed.

"You don't understand," Leo said, his voice tinged with frustration. "This is how business works. We make these moves to grow. To ensure survival. There's no other way. We've reached a point where we need to make bold moves, and this merger—this merger is everything."

Claire shook her head, her expression softening into something that felt almost like sadness. "No, Leo. You don't understand." She took a step closer, her gaze unwavering. "This isn't just about business. This is about people—real people. Thousands of people who are going to lose their jobs because of this deal. Families that are going to be torn apart. You can't just brush that aside."

Leo felt a pang in his chest, something he hadn't expected. A flicker of guilt, of uncertainty. But he quickly dismissed it. "You're being emotional. This is a necessary part of growth. You can't make an omelette without cracking a few eggs."

Claire's face reddened with a mix of anger and helplessness. "I'm not being emotional. I'm being human. These are people, Leo. Not just numbers on a spreadsheet. And you're too blinded by your ambition to see it. You're willing to sacrifice your values—and our community—for a bigger pay check and a higher status. Is that really what you want? To be the king of a kingdom built on the backs of the people who've helped you get here?"

Leo's pulse quickened. He could feel the walls closing in, the suffocating weight of Claire's words pressing against him. He wanted to argue, to convince her that this was the only way forward, that they had no other choice. But for the first time in years, Leo found himself at a loss for words.

"You don't get it, do you?" Claire whispered, the anger fading into a sorrowful resignation. "You've become so consumed by this drive to be the biggest, the best, that you've lost sight of everything else. Your integrity. Your family. Our future. And now you're going to erase the livelihood of thousands of people for what? A larger corporate footprint? A few extra zeros on your pay check?"

Leo's silence stretched between them, heavy and suffocating. He could feel the truth of her words gnawing at him, but the weight of his decision was already too heavy to bear. He had made his choice. It was done.

"I can't stop it now," Leo said, his voice flat, distant. "The deal is already in motion. There's no turning back."

Claire took a step back, the hurt evident on her face. "Then you've already made your choice, Leo. And I'm not sure I can live with that."

She turned and walked toward the door, her back straight, her steps deliberate. Leo stood frozen, watching her leave, the finality of the moment settling in like a cold breeze. The empire he had fought so hard to build, the empire that had come to define him, was no longer just his. It was built on the sacrifices of others—sacrifices he could no longer ignore.

In the quiet that followed, Leo Harper was left alone with his decisions, and for the first time, the bright lights of success felt dimmer than ever.

CHAPTER FOUR

The door slammed behind Leo with a finality that echoed down the hallway of their high-rise apartment. His heart pounded in his chest, the anger still burning, but beneath it, something darker was beginning to grow—a gnawing emptiness that he couldn't shake. Claire's words had stung. They had lodged themselves deep inside him, like splinters that refused to be removed, each one digging into him as he stormed out into the cold New York night.

The city sprawled before him, indifferent to his pain. The streets pulsed with life, the glow of neon signs and the hum of late-night traffic creating a rhythm that Leo had once thrived in. He had always felt invincible here, a king in the concrete jungle, unshaken by anything or anyone. But tonight, the city felt alien—hostile even. The cold wind cut through his suit, sharp and biting, as if it were an extension of the icy silence that had settled between him and Claire.

Leo didn't know where he was going, or if he even cared. He walked aimlessly, letting his feet guide him, the noise of the city fading into the background as his mind spun in circles. He had always prided himself on his ability to make decisions, to control the direction of his life with precision. But tonight, for the first time in years, he felt lost.

As he passed a row of gleaming skyscrapers, he found himself looking up at the walls of glass and steel, the reflection of the city's lights creating a shimmering glow.

These buildings, these monuments to ambition, were a testament to everything he had worked for. Yet tonight, they felt like towering reminders of what he had sacrificed.

Was it worth it? The question lingered in his mind; its answer as elusive as the wind that whipped through the streets.

Leo's footsteps carried him through the city's maze, past the bustle of Times Square and the shadows of Central Park. He didn't stop. He couldn't. The cold, the noise, the sheer vastness of the city were the only things that felt tangible. Everything else—his business, his family, his life—felt like it was slipping through his fingers.

The argument with Claire replayed in his mind like a movie he couldn't escape. She had accused him of losing sight of what really mattered. Of becoming so consumed by his own ambition that he had forgotten about the people who loved him. And she was right. He had always believed that success was the answer—that if he could just get to the top, everything else would fall into place. But now, in the quiet of the night, he began to question everything.

The city was alive, teeming with possibilities, yet Leo felt disconnected from it all. His empire was vast, his influence undeniable, but none of it seemed to matter anymore. He could hear Claire's voice in his head, her words echoing through the silence: *"Is this really what you want? To be the king of a kingdom built on the backs of the people who've helped you get here?"*

He stopped at the edge of a street corner, staring out at the neon signs that flickered in the distance. A familiar ache twisted in his chest as he thought about Claire—her quiet strength, the way she had always been his anchor. But now, it felt like she was slipping away from him. And he couldn't seem to find a way to stop it.

Was it worth it?

He had asked himself that question before, but never like this. Never with the weight of his own choices pressing down on him. He had spent so many years building something that, in the grand scheme of things, didn't seem to matter. The deal with the tech giant was just another step in a long line of moves that promised to make him richer, more powerful, more untouchable. But at what cost?

Leo's gaze drifted to the streetlights, their glow soft and distant against the night sky. They reminded him of the warmth he had once shared with Claire, the life they had built together before everything had become so... impersonal. Now, even his marriage felt like something he was managing rather than living.

He thought of the people who worked for him, the thousands of lives that had been affected by his decisions. The layoffs that would come with the merger—what would that mean for them? Were they just numbers to him? People whose lives could be shattered so that he could rise higher?

For the first time in a long time, Leo felt a pang of guilt, of regret. He had been so focused on climbing higher, on reaching the pinnacle of success, that he hadn't stopped to ask whether it was worth the cost. Was it worth losing his family? His sense of self? Was it worth sacrificing the very values that had brought him to the top in the first place?

The sound of a car horn jolted him out of his thoughts. He was standing at the edge of a busy intersection now, cars speeding by, their headlights blurring in the night. Leo took a step back, his mind still racing. He needed to clear his head. He needed to make sense of all this.

Without thinking, he turned and started walking again, his pace quickening as if he were trying to outrun the storm inside his mind. The city seemed endless, its streets twisting and turning like a maze that had no exit. Leo couldn't help but wonder if this was how his life had become—an endless pursuit of something he couldn't quite name, a journey that had no destination.

He passed a small park; the benches empty and silent in the cold. The trees, stripped bare of leaves, stood like sentinels in the dark. Leo sat on one of the benches, his breath fogging in the air as he leaned forward, elbows resting on his knees. The weight of the decision to merge with the tech giant pressed down on him harder now. The loss of jobs. The destruction of families. The feeling of powerlessness that had started to creep in.

Leo closed his eyes, trying to push away the guilt that threatened to swallow him whole. He had always believed that success meant freedom—that with enough power, enough wealth, he could shape the world in his image. But now, as he sat there in the cold, he realized how fragile that world had become. The empire he had built was a house of cards, held together by the very people he had pushed aside.

A gust of wind blew through the park, and Leo shivered, pulling his coat tighter around himself. He couldn't remember the last time he had felt truly at peace. The relentless pace of his life, the constant demand to perform, to be the best—it had consumed him. He had become a slave to his own ambition.

For the first time in years, Leo felt a flicker of something different. Not the rush of success or the thrill of power, but something slower, deeper. A question that he couldn't ignore anymore.

What is the price of success?

The answer eluded him, just as the answers to all his other questions had. But in that moment, sitting on a cold bench in the heart of New York, Leo Harper began to realize that his success might not be enough to save him. And that realization, more than any deal, any merger, or any financial triumph, was the one that scared him the most.

The city stretched out before him, its lights bright and endless, but for the first time, Leo wasn't sure he wanted to be a part of it anymore.

CHAPTER FIVE

Leo had no particular destination in mind when he found himself wandering through another park, his steps slow and aimless. The cold had seeped deep into his bones, but it wasn't just the weather that made him feel so hollow. It was the weight of his life, the choices he had made, and the widening chasm between what he had achieved and what he truly wanted.

He passed by joggers and couples wrapped in scarves, each seemingly in their own world, and for a moment, Leo almost wished he could be one of them—someone who hadn't spent every waking hour chasing after an ideal that now felt increasingly empty. The park, with its stillness and quiet beauty, seemed like an oasis from the storm of his thoughts. He found a bench and sat down, trying to center himself, to regain some semblance of clarity. But just as he closed his eyes and let the breeze wash over him, something unusual caught his attention.

A small crowd had gathered a few yards away, their faces turned toward a man standing in the center. At first, Leo assumed it was just another street performer or motivational speaker, but there was something about this group that seemed different. The people gathered weren't holding phones or checking their watches; they were *listening.*

Leo, intrigued despite himself, stood up and moved closer.

In the center of the group stood a monk, draped in simple orange robes, his face calm and serene. His presence seemed to fill the space around him in a way Leo couldn't quite explain. The crowd, a diverse mix of young professionals, students, and older people, was silent, hanging on to every word the monk spoke. There was no stage, no microphone, just the soft hum of the city in the background, but in that moment, the monk's voice was the only thing that mattered.

"Most of us," the monk said, his voice deep but gentle, "spend our lives chasing things that we think will bring us happiness. Wealth. Success. Power. We believe these things will fill the emptiness within us. But what we fail to see is that the more we accumulate, the more our desires grow, and the more we suffer. The mind, constantly craving, never finds rest."

Leo felt a pang of discomfort as the monk's words seemed to reach into him, as though he were speaking directly to his heart. He had spent so much of his life chasing success, thinking it would be the key to everything—happiness, fulfillment, peace. But in the hollow moments between meetings, in the silence of his apartment, he had felt none of that. Instead, he felt increasingly burdened, as though the more he achieved, the more he lost.

The monk continued, unfazed by the skeptical looks some in the crowd might have been exchanging. "True happiness," he said, his eyes sweeping over the gathering, "is not something to be found in external things. It is a state of being. A quiet, unshakable peace that comes from within. And to find that peace, we must learn to tame the mind, to free ourselves from the endless cycle of desires and attachments."

Leo couldn't help himself. He stepped forward, his curiosity getting the best of him.

"Are you saying we should all just give up on everything?" Leo called out, his voice laced with disbelief.

The monk turned toward him, his gaze steady and kind. "Not everything, my friend. Only the things that enslave you. It is not the world or the people in it that cause suffering, but our attachment to them. Our constant craving for more. We must learn to release the grip of these desires to find true freedom."

Leo frowned, feeling the skepticism rise in him. He had built his entire life on the pursuit of success. Everything he had was because of his drive, his ambition. "But how do you expect us to live in this world and not want more? Isn't that what drives us? What motivates us to succeed, to grow, to push forward?"

The monk smiled, a quiet, knowing smile. "Yes, ambition can be a force for good, but it must be guided by wisdom. When we pursue success without awareness, we become slaves to our own desires. We begin to measure our worth by what we have or how others see us. And in that process, we lose sight of who we truly are."

Leo's mind raced. There was something in the monk's words that resonated with him, something deep inside that wanted to believe it, but he couldn't shake his doubts. The world he knew—the world of corporate deals, mergers, power—seemed so far removed from the simplicity the monk was describing. How could letting go of ambition be the answer?

But then, Leo caught a glimpse of the people around him—their faces, not tense or hurried, but relaxed, peaceful. They were listening, not for answers, but for a deeper truth. A truth that felt almost foreign to him, yet strangely inviting.

"Does this peace," Leo asked, his voice softer now, "mean we just stop trying? Stop striving for more?"

The monk shook his head, his smile gentle. "It means we stop fighting against what is. It means we live with intention, not in reaction. Strive for excellence, but not out of fear, or the need to prove yourself. Strive because it brings you joy, because it aligns with your true self. But never lose sight of the fact that you are already whole, already complete. You do not need external validation to be at peace."

Leo felt the words wash over him, stirring something deep within—a part of him that had been buried under years of stress and ambition. He could feel his chest tightening as the monk's words seemed to chip away at the walls he had built around himself.

The monk spoke again, his voice a soft beacon in the cold night air. "The true test of a man is not in what he has, but in what he is able to let go of."

Leo stood there, his mind racing as the crowd began to disperse. The words echoed in his ears long after the monk had finished speaking. He had come here expecting nothing more than a passing distraction, but something inside him had shifted. It was subtle, almost imperceptible, but undeniable.

As Leo walked away, his mind still swirling, he couldn't help but feel that he had just encountered something far more valuable than any business deal, any merger, or any amount of wealth.

He had encountered a glimpse of a different way of living—a way of being that was not defined by what you achieved or what you possessed. A way of living that, for the first time in his life, seemed like it might actually offer the peace he had been searching for all along.

The monk's words echoed in Leo's mind as he disappeared into the night: *You do not need external validation to be at peace.*

Leo wasn't sure what had just happened, but one thing was certain—his life, and everything he had worked for, would never be the same again.

CHAPTER SIX

The cold grip of New York's night air still lingered on Leo's skin as he walked away from the park. The monk's words continued to reverberate in his mind, like echoes bouncing off the walls of his consciousness. *You do not need external validation to be at peace.* The sentence was simple, but its impact was profound, unsettling. It struck him in a way nothing ever had, causing a crack in the armor of his beliefs, a sliver of doubt he couldn't easily dismiss.

Leo Harper, the multimillionaire CEO, had built his life on the principles of control, success, and results. He had never been one for spirituality, let alone philosophy that questioned the very foundation of what he thought he knew. He was an atheist, a man of reason and logic. He believed in the power of the mind, but only as it related to tangible, measurable success. Spiritual talk, the pursuit of inner peace, seemed like a distraction. A luxury reserved for those who couldn't handle the harsh realities of the world.

Yet as he sat in his sleek penthouse that night, staring out at the glittering skyline, something inside him stirred—something more than just curiosity. He had dismissed the monk's words earlier, brushed them off with a cynicism that had always shielded him from anything that felt intangible or unquantifiable. But now, those same words crept back into his thoughts, gnawing at him, making him question the very life he had built.

The restless, never-satisfied hunger he had felt for years now seemed to pulse within him with more intensity than ever before. He had everything: money, power, influence—but none of it had ever quelled the emptiness that gnawed at his soul. He had spent a lifetime filling the void with acquisitions, deals, and victories, yet it had never been enough. And now, a simple monk in the middle of a New York park had pointed out something he had known all along but had refused to acknowledge: *The mind was restless, and it could never be satisfied by external things.*

Leo leaned back on his couch, his thoughts swirling like a storm. He hadn't realized how tired he was until now—tired of running, tired of chasing after something that always seemed just out of reach. His mind was a constant buzz, always calculating, always striving. The endless list of to-do's, the demands of the business, the constant pressure to perform—it was exhausting. The hunger, the thirst for more, was never quenched, no matter how many deals he closed or how many people admired him.

He thought back to the monk's words, *True happiness is not something to be found in external things.* It had sounded foreign at the time, but now, it almost made sense. Leo had spent his entire life looking for happiness in the wrong places. In the trophies of his success, in the applause of others, in the validation of the world. But it had all been fleeting, as temporary as the sparkle of a diamond in the sun.

It wasn't just the success he had craved—it was the sense of peace, the sense of being in control, that he had mistaken for happiness. But peace, the monk had said, wasn't something to be fought for or grasped. It was already within him. He just had to quiet the noise of the restless mind to find it.

But how could he? How could he, Leo Harper, the man who had conquered the business world with sheer will and determination, suddenly surrender to this unfamiliar notion of inner peace?

His thoughts were interrupted by a knock at the door. He stood up, almost mechanically, as if on autopilot, and opened it to find a messenger standing in the hallway, holding an envelope addressed to him.

Without a word, Leo took the envelope, thanked the man, and closed the door behind him. The heavy weight of the envelope felt strange in his hand, as if it contained something far more important than any business correspondence or legal paperwork he had ever received. He sat back down, the envelope still in his hands, hesitating for a moment before tearing it open.

Inside was a letter, handwritten in elegant, flowing script. The handwriting was unfamiliar, but the name at the top struck him immediately.

Swami Ananda.

The letter read:

"Dear Leo Harper,

It was a joy to meet you in the park the other night. I sensed that you were searching for something beyond what the world offers. We all search, whether we know it or not. The mind, restless and full of desires, is the cause of much of our suffering. It never rests, always chasing something—success, recognition, control—but these pursuits only deepen the craving, never satisfy it. True peace can only be found when the mind is quieted. To quiet the mind, we must first recognize its nature and then release the attachments that bind us. This is not an easy task, but it is the only path to true freedom.

I invite you to visit me at the ashram in the Himalayas, where we will explore the mind and its restless tendencies in greater depth. I believe you are ready to begin this journey, Leo, though it may take you farther than you imagine.

Yours in peace,

Swami Ananda"

Leo sat in stunned silence, the words of the letter sinking in slowly. A part of him wanted to laugh, to dismiss it as nonsense, to tear the letter up and forget about the monk altogether. But another part of him—the part that had been quietly restless for years, the part that was seeking something more than what money and power could offer—felt an undeniable pull.

A trip to the Himalayas. An invitation from a man he had met only once, a man whose teachings had shaken him in a way he had never experienced. Leo had been many places in his life, but never somewhere like this—never somewhere that promised to confront him with the very thing he had spent so long avoiding: the truth of his own mind.

Could he really go? Could he, a man of reason and logic, step into a world of spirituality that seemed so alien to him? Could he trust this monk, whose words had felt like a lifeline, despite the skepticism he still carried?

Leo took a deep breath and looked out the window at the sprawling city below. The night lights twinkled like stars, each one a reminder of the empire he had built, the legacy he was creating. But none of it mattered. None of it filled the void. None of it brought him the peace he sought.

He folded the letter and placed it on the table, his hands trembling slightly. For the first time in his life, he felt a choice that was unlike any business decision he had ever made. It was a choice to surrender, to explore a path he had never considered, to let go of the relentless pursuit of success and discover something deeper.

The restlessness inside him had not disappeared, but it had shifted. It had become a yearning, an invitation to seek something more—something beyond the mind, beyond the chase.

Leo Harper knew, deep down, that he couldn't ignore this call. The path ahead was uncertain, and perhaps, just maybe, it was the only one that could offer the peace he had been seeking for so long.

CHAPTER SEVEN

Leo sat in his office, staring blankly at the stack of paperwork in front of him. The world outside, the one he had meticulously built with years of effort, ambition, and sacrifice, seemed to blur into the background. The hum of his phone, the emails flooding his inbox, the calls demanding his attention—all of it felt so distant, so insignificant. The glossy promise of another successful merger, the accumulation of wealth, the carefully orchestrated life he had led—all of it seemed hollow now, like a carefully constructed facade.

He had never considered himself impulsive. He was a man who calculated, who analyzed every possibility before making a move. But something had shifted inside him. The letter from Swami Ananda, with its invitation to the ashram in the Himalayas, had awakened something deep within Leo—a restlessness, a yearning for something beyond the world he knew. Something that couldn't be quantified, measured, or achieved.

His mind raced, torn between the responsibilities that awaited him—the finalization of a massive deal that would solidify his company's dominance in the tech world—and the pull he felt toward the unknown. He glanced at the calendar on his desk, where the dates of crucial meetings and events were neatly marked. The world demanded his attention. His employees, his investors, his wife—they all depended on him.

But then, like a sudden gust of wind, clarity swept over him. What was he running from? What was he so afraid to confront? His entire life had been driven by external validation—money, power, success—but none of it had brought him the peace he was desperately seeking. He realized, with a jolt, that he had been living in a perpetual state of distraction. Always running, always achieving, always proving, but never stopping to ask himself *why*.

His hands shook as he reached for the letter again, rereading Swami Ananda's words. *True peace can only be found when the mind is quieted. To quiet the mind, we must first recognize its nature and then release the attachments that bind us.* Leo had dismissed these words in the beginning, but now, they seemed like a beacon in the fog of his life. He needed to see this journey through, to confront whatever was lying on the other side of his restless mind.

He stood up abruptly, his chair scraping against the floor. His heart beat a little faster as the realization hit him—he was going to do it. He was going to leave it all behind, at least for a while. The business. The meetings. The endless pursuit of success. All of it could wait.

With a deep breath, Leo grabbed his jacket and headed for the door. His assistant, Sarah, looked up from her desk, her expression a mix of confusion and concern. "Leo? Where are you going? You've got back-to-back meetings this afternoon, and the merger—"

"I know," Leo interrupted, his voice steady but filled with an unexpected determination. "Cancel them all."

Sarah's eyes widened. "Cancel them? Sir, we're talking about a deal that could make or break—"

Leo held up his hand, silencing her. "I know what I'm doing, Sarah. Please, just... handle it. I need to step away for a while."

Without waiting for a response, he turned and walked out of the office, the familiar hum of the building now a distant noise in his ears. As he stepped into the elevator, he realized that this wasn't just another business decision—it was the beginning of something new, something that would take him far beyond the realm of numbers and spreadsheets.

He didn't know what lay ahead, only that it was a journey he had to take. There were no guarantees, no promises of success. But for the first time in years, Leo felt something he hadn't felt in a long time: a flicker of hope.

CHAPTER EIGHT

The moment Leo stepped off the plane in New Delhi, the assault of sensations hit him immediately. The air was thick, humid, and full of life. The chaos of the airport was palpable—people rushing in every direction, the loud, staccato sound of announcements in a language he barely understood, and the mix of scents: incense, spices, diesel fumes. It was a sensory overload. Here, in India, the world felt raw, unrefined, alive in a way his polished New York life had never been.

His finely tailored suit felt foreign to the heat, its fabric clinging to his skin as though mocking his effort to remain in control. The familiar hum of his corporate empire—the quiet of his Manhattan penthouse, the hum of the boardroom, the precision of his life—seemed impossibly distant now, as if he had stepped into a completely different world.

Leo tried to hold his composure, but it was hard. In a place like this, where everything seemed to pulse with unpredictability and vitality, he felt like a stranger. The streets outside the airport were a blur of movement—cars honking, rickshaws weaving through traffic, pedestrians walking with a calm certainty he didn't quite understand. Everything here was different, so different from the life of control and order he had created for himself.

He stood still for a moment, trying to make sense of the overwhelming noise and bustle surrounding him. The hum of the city, the sheer volume of people, felt like a stark contrast to the controlled silence he had so carefully curated back home. But here, none of it mattered. No one cared about his success, his power, or his position in the world. The world continued to move, indifferent to his presence.

A young man in simple clothing approached him with a polite smile. "Sir, are you Leo Harper?" he asked, his English accented but clear.

"Yes," Leo replied, nodding, trying to appear as though he had control over his surroundings. "I'm Leo. You're here to take me to the ashram?"

The young man, Raj, confirmed and led him to a waiting car. As they drove through the streets of Delhi, Leo could not shake the unease growing in his chest. He had prepared for this. He had read up on the culture, learned a few words of Hindi, and mentally braced himself for what he imagined India would be like. But none of that had prepared him for this—this overwhelming sensory experience, this world where his usual tools of control and precision didn't apply.

The car weaved through the crowded streets, and Leo observed the stark contrast between his world and the one he was now entering. The wealth he had amassed seemed irrelevant here. The gleaming skyscrapers of New York were a distant memory now, and he felt a profound disconnect. The streets were filled with people—some in brightly colored saris, others dressed in traditional robes. Vendors shouted about their wares, selling everything from jewelry to fresh fruit.

But in the midst of the chaos, Leo noticed something unexpected—contentment. Despite the madness of the city, there was a calmness about the people. A quiet acceptance. It was a stark contrast to his life, one where he had spent years building a perfect empire that was, in the end, hollow.

His thoughts were interrupted by Raj's voice. "We're about to leave the city now. Just a short drive, and then a walk to the ashram."

As the car moved away from the city center, the landscape began to change. The city's chaos faded, replaced by winding roads lined with trees, small villages, and open fields. The noise of the city was slowly replaced by a softer rhythm—the occasional hum of a passing car, the chirp of birds, the rustle of leaves in the wind. And with it, Leo's unease began to shift slightly.

Still, the discomfort lingered. How could he, a man who had spent years climbing the corporate ladder, feel so out of place? How could he, a man of power and influence, feel so small in this land where his wealth meant nothing? His thoughts turned inward, spiraling into a familiar place of doubt and uncertainty.

What had driven him to leave it all behind? The merger, the business, the promises of continued success—it had all been left behind for this. But for what? He had come to India seeking peace, seeking answers to questions he had buried for so long. Yet, as he sat in the back of the car, surrounded by a world so different from the one he had known, the fear of the unknown gnawed at him.

The car slowed as it approached a small village, the houses scattered along narrow, winding streets. Raj pointed to a narrow path that led up into the foothills of the Himalayas.

"Just a short walk from here," Raj said. "The ashram is on the hill."

Leo nodded but felt a flutter of hesitation. What had he really come here for? Was the peace he was searching for truly to be found here, in this strange, foreign place? Could Swami Ananda, a man far removed from the world of suits, mergers, and tech giants, really offer him the answers he needed?

The path before him looked steep, winding through the hills toward the distant peaks of the Himalayas. Leo took a deep breath, feeling the coolness of the air as he stepped out of the car. There was no turning back now. He had come too far.

As he began the short walk toward the ashram, his finely pressed suit and shiny shoes felt heavier than ever. It wasn't just the weight of his clothing, but the weight of his past—the life he had left behind. It seemed to press down on him, but with each step, the pressure began to ease, just a little.

The village behind him faded into the distance, the sounds of life quieter now. His thoughts quieted too, as the stillness of the mountains began to settle around him. For the first time in days, Leo felt something stir within him—a sense of possibility, of hope, even if it was faint. The journey ahead wasn't about what he had left behind, but what he could find now.

The path up the hill grew steeper, but Leo didn't mind. He focused on his breath, on the rhythm of his steps, and for the first time in a long while, he felt his mind begin to settle. Perhaps, just perhaps, this was the beginning of something new. Something deeper.

At the top of the hill, the ashram appeared—modest, simple, but surrounded by a serene garden that felt sacred. Swami Ananda waited for him there, calm and steady, like a force of nature in his stillness.

"Welcome, Leo," the Swami said softly. "You have traveled far to be here. But the real journey begins now, within you."

Leo stood before him, his heart still racing from the journey, but something inside him stirred. He had arrived, and with it, he realized the true journey was not about the destination. It was about the process of seeking. And finally, he had begun to understand what he had come here for.

CHAPTER NINE

The morning light filtered through the ancient trees that surrounded the ashram, casting soft shadows on the stone path that led to the small meditation hall. Leo stood before it, the weight of the decision he had made pressing heavily on his chest.

Leo was no stranger to discipline or persistence. He had built his empire on those very traits. But this—this was different. The world of business, with its endless meetings, power struggles, and transactions, had been tangible. The goal had always been clear: success, money, control. But here, in the quiet of the Himalayas, there were no visible markers of progress, no financial targets to hit, no deals to close. The goal was internal, abstract—a control of something he had never fully understood: the mind.

As Leo stepped inside the meditation hall, the cool, fragrant air of incense settled over him like a blanket. The room was sparsely decorated, with only a few mats scattered across the wooden floor. In the far corner, Swami Ananda sat in quiet contemplation, his eyes closed, his posture straight, his breath slow and steady. Leo approached, the sound of his footsteps muffled by the thick matting.

"Good morning, Leo," the Swami greeted him, his voice soft but unwavering, as though the very air around him was imbued with calm. "Are you ready for your first lesson?"

Leo nodded, his heart racing slightly. He had read about meditation and controlling the mind in countless books, but reading was one thing—experiencing it was another.

Swami Ananda motioned to the mat beside him. "Sit with me. Let us begin."

Leo lowered himself to the mat, cross-legged, his posture stiff and unnatural. He tried to recall the lessons he had read about sitting with a straight back, about focusing on the breath. He was determined to make this work. His empire had been built on discipline and control, and he would approach this challenge with the same level of commitment.

"Close your eyes, Leo," Swami Ananda instructed, his voice gentle, yet firm. "Focus on your breath. Feel it as it enters and leaves your body."

Leo took a deep breath, inhaling through his nose, filling his lungs with the cool air. He exhaled slowly, the rush of air a reminder of the simple act of breathing, something so natural, yet so often overlooked. He focused on the rhythm—inhale, exhale. It felt easy at first, but soon his mind began to wander.

A sudden thought struck him—he needed to check his phone. What was happening back at the office? Was the merger still on track? Was his team handling things without him? His breath faltered, and his mind began to race with the weight of all the decisions he had left behind. The tension in his shoulders grew, and he found himself opening his eyes, glancing around the room, trying to ground himself back in the moment.

"Leo," Swami Ananda's voice broke through the noise of his thoughts. "What are you running from?"

Leo stiffened, surprised by the question. He hadn't expected the Swami to address him directly during the meditation. "I'm not running from anything," Leo replied, though he knew that wasn't entirely true. He had left everything behind—his company, his ambitions—but the thoughts still followed him, like shadows.

The Swami's eyes opened slowly, and he regarded Leo with an almost imperceptible smile. "The mind does not stop, Leo. It wanders like a wild river, pulling you in many directions. But you can learn to calm it. You can learn to control it. Just as a mountain climber ascends the peak with persistence and steady effort, so too must you train the mind. Each step is an effort. Each breath, a reminder of the path you are on."

Leo felt a flicker of understanding, though the words still seemed distant. A mountain climber. The metaphor was simple, but it felt profound in the stillness of the room. Leo had always viewed challenges as obstacles to be conquered, but controlling his mind? That seemed like an impossible task. The thoughts he had spent years suppressing now surged to the forefront, clamoring for attention.

Swami Ananda continued. "The mind is like the mountain. The summit is stillness, peace, and clarity. But to reach it, you must climb. And the climb is not easy. It is fraught with distractions, fatigue, and doubt. But with each step, you grow stronger. With each breath, you build your focus."

Leo closed his eyes again, trying to steady himself. He could feel the tension in his shoulders, the weight of his thoughts, but this time, he tried to focus on his breath, on the steady rise and fall of his chest. Inhale. Exhale. The rhythm was the same, but this time, Leo tried to imagine it as the movement of a climber scaling a treacherous peak. Every breath, a small victory. Every moment of stillness, a step closer to the summit.

The thoughts continued to intrude. The merger. The future of his company. His family. The ever-present pressure of his past life. But with each distraction, Leo tried to return to the rhythm of his breath, as though it were a rope, pulling him upward, steadying him against the pull of the distractions.

Minutes passed, though it felt like hours. Slowly, Leo began to feel a subtle shift. His body, stiff and tense, started to relax. The incessant noise of his thoughts began to quiet, not completely, but enough that he could focus on the simple act of breathing. He wasn't there yet—he hadn't reached the summit—but he had taken the first steps. And that, he realized, was the point.

Swami Ananda's voice broke the silence again. "The mind is always moving, always restless. But just as the climber does not abandon the mountain halfway up, you must not abandon the mind when it wanders. Each time you return to the breath, you strengthen your focus. Each time you regain control, you climb higher."

Leo opened his eyes, looking at the Swami with newfound clarity. It wasn't about achieving instant peace or perfect control. It was about the effort, the persistence, the understanding that every distraction was an opportunity to return to stillness.

Swami Ananda smiled softly, as though he could read Leo's thoughts. "It is a journey, Leo. A slow, steady journey. And like climbing a mountain, you will find that the summit is not the end, but the beginning of a deeper peace."

Leo nodded, feeling the weight of the lesson settle within him. This was only the beginning of a much longer climb. But for the first time in a long while, he felt a glimmer of hope.

CHAPTER TEN

The days at the ashram bled together in a quiet rhythm—each morning marked by the rise of the sun, each evening by the calm descent of twilight. Leo had been here for nearly a week now, and while the scenery was breathtaking, and the air peaceful, he had begun to feel the weight of his inner turmoil. The silence he had sought was quickly filled with the noise of his own thoughts. The more he tried to quiet them, the louder they became. He couldn't escape the sense that he was slowly unraveling.

On the surface, everything appeared serene. Leo meditated in the mornings, sat with Swami Ananda in the evenings, and spent the rest of the time wandering the grounds, lost in thought. Yet underneath this outward calm, something was stirring. It wasn't just his mind—it was his very self. The life he had left behind, the empire he had built, the ambitions that had once driven him—none of it seemed to matter here. Yet, without those things, who was he?

It was the evening of the seventh day when Swami Ananda spoke again, his voice calm and measured as ever.

"Leo," the Swami said, his gaze steady, "you've been struggling. Your mind is scattered, and your heart is torn between old desires and new understandings. But this struggle is the beginning of your growth."

Leo nodded, feeling a pang of frustration. "I want to believe that, Swami. But I can't seem to focus. Every thought, every emotion, just pulls me in a different direction. I feel like I'm fighting myself—like my mind is at war with my soul."

Swami Ananda regarded him with a quiet wisdom. "This is the nature of the human mind, Leo. It is restless, fragmented. The thoughts and emotions you feel are like wild horses, pulling you in all directions. But you, Leo, must be the rider, not the horse. To be the rider, you must first strengthen your will."

Leo's brow furrowed. "Strengthen my will? But how? Every time I try to concentrate, I'm distracted. Every time I make progress, I fall back into the same patterns of doubt and desire."

The Swami smiled gently. "Strengthening the will is not easy. It requires discipline and focus. But more than that, it requires aligning your actions with something higher—something beyond the fleeting desires of the body and the ego. You must learn to master your mind, not through force, but through understanding."

Leo felt the weight of those words. He had spent his entire life chasing after external success—money, power, recognition—but here, in the stillness of the ashram, none of it seemed to matter. The life he had built felt empty, his soul adrift. He had thought that success would bring him peace, but now, it only felt like a distant mirage.

Swami Ananda continued, "The mind, like a sword, is dull and fragmented when it is undisciplined. But with consistent effort, you can sharpen it. With each moment of focus, with each act of will, the sword becomes stronger, more precise. Your will, Leo, is like that sword—it will become sharper with time, with discipline."

Leo sat up straighter, trying to absorb the depth of the Swami's words. "So, you're saying that the mind can be sharpened? That I can actually learn to control it?"

"Yes," the Swami replied. "But first, you must understand that the will is not separate from the mind. It is a part of it. Strengthening the will is not about forcing control over the mind. It is about aligning the mind with a higher purpose, a higher goal. When your actions are guided by a greater sense of purpose, the distractions lose their power over you."

Leo closed his eyes and let the words settle in. Aligning the mind with a higher purpose. It sounded simple enough, but the more he thought about it, the more he realized how little he had ever aligned his actions with anything deeper than success. The fleeting pleasures of victory, of power, had driven him for so long. But now, sitting in the quiet of the ashram, he wondered what would happen if he could truly redirect that energy toward something greater—something more meaningful.

The Swami placed a hand on Leo's shoulder, his touch grounding and steady. "Imagine, Leo, that you are holding a sword. The blade is dull, not sharp, and it is hard to wield. It takes constant effort, consistent honing, for the sword to become sharp. The more you work at it, the more you practice, the better you become at using it. This is how you must treat your will—the sword of determination. You must hone it every day."

Leo felt a flicker of understanding. "Like a mountain climber who sharpens his tools before the climb. Or like an athlete who trains daily to build strength."

"Exactly," the Swami affirmed. "Your will is your most powerful tool, but it must be strengthened through consistent practice. Your thoughts, your actions, your desires—they will always be there, pulling you in many directions. But the sharper your will becomes, the more able you will be to direct them toward your highest purpose."

Leo sat in silence, considering the metaphor. Sharpening the will was like sharpening a sword—it wasn't a quick fix. It wasn't a sudden, dramatic change. It was a slow, steady process that required effort, discipline, and above all, focus.

The lesson was clear, though difficult to grasp: Willpower was not something that could be summoned at will. It was something that had to be cultivated, honed, and sharpened. And just as a sword became sharper with each stroke of the whetstone, Leo's will would become stronger through each act of focus, each moment of discipline.

"Willpower is not an isolated force," Swami Ananda continued. "It is connected to your values, your purpose. When your will is aligned with your highest goal, the distractions of the world no longer control you. The fleeting pleasures of the ego lose their grip, and you begin to experience true freedom."

Leo's heart quickened as a new understanding began to take root. The world he had built was rooted in fleeting pleasures—money, success, power—but here, in the stillness of the ashram, he was learning that there was something deeper, something more lasting. It wasn't about controlling his mind through force. It was about redirecting his energy toward something higher.

"Do not rush the process, Leo," Swami Ananda cautioned, sensing his restlessness. "Strengthening your will requires patience. It requires persistence. But just as a sword becomes sharper with every stroke, so too will your will become stronger with every conscious choice you make. Your actions, aligned with purpose, will guide you to the strength you seek."

Leo nodded, feeling a sense of clarity begin to settle within him. It wouldn't be easy. The struggle was far from over. But now, he understood what he had to do. He had to sharpen his will, one decision at a time, one moment of focus at a time. And as he did, he would begin to carve a path toward something far more meaningful than success.

He stood, slowly and deliberately, and bowed to the Swami. "Thank you, Swami. I will begin my practice. I will sharpen the sword."

Swami Ananda smiled; his eyes gleaming with quiet approval. "The sword is already within you, Leo. You need only to learn how to wield it."

CHAPTER ELEVEN

The days in the ashram seemed to stretch on endlessly for Leo. The quiet, the stillness—it was both a balm and a challenge. He had begun to notice changes in himself, subtle yet undeniable. He was no longer as restless, no longer driven by the same unrelenting need to conquer every task. There was space now—space to breathe, to think, and to feel. But despite these shifts, there was still something elusive. A deeper understanding, a more profound sense of control, seemed just beyond his reach.

It was on the tenth day that Swami Ananda spoke again, this time with an urgency that Leo hadn't yet experienced. The Swami had been guiding him with patient wisdom, but today, there was a fire in his voice, a sense of gravity in his presence.

"Leo," the Swami began, his voice calm but carrying the weight of truth, "we have spoken of willpower, of discipline. But now, you must understand what is truly at stake in controlling your mind. It is not merely about overcoming distractions. It is about the very essence of your life."

Leo leaned forward, his mind alert. The Swami had his full attention.

"Without control over the mind," Swami Ananda continued, "life becomes chaotic. It becomes like a ship without a rudder, adrift in a storm. You are tossed and turned by every wave, every thought, every desire. But when you control your mind, you become the master of your own course. You become the one who steers the ship, who directs the flow of your life."

Leo's eyes widened as the Swami spoke. The metaphor was simple, but it struck him with the force of truth. A controlled mind, he realized, was the key to everything he sought—peace, purpose, clarity. Without it, life would continue to spiral, driven by the currents of impulse and desire. But with it, he could find direction. He could steer his life toward something greater.

"Think of your mind as the steering wheel of a car," the Swami said, his gaze piercing through Leo as though he could see straight into his thoughts. "When you grip the wheel firmly, you can drive forward with purpose. You can follow a clear path. But when your hands are loose, when you let your mind wander aimlessly, you risk losing control. The car may veer off course, crash into obstacles, or drive in circles. Without direction, you are lost."

Leo closed his eyes, imagining himself behind the wheel of a car. He could see it vividly in his mind: the open road, the endless possibilities, but also the danger of losing control. Without focus, the car could easily veer off the road, crashing into the unknown. It was the same with his mind—if he didn't take control, he risked being swept away by distractions, desires, and the chaos of his thoughts.

Swami Ananda continued, "Controlling the mind is not about suppressing your thoughts or emotions. It is about learning to steer them, to direct them towards a higher purpose. When you let the mind run wild, it leads you astray. It pulls you toward fleeting pleasures, momentary satisfactions that ultimately leave you feeling empty. But when you learn to steer it, to focus it on what truly matters, it becomes a powerful force for growth, peace, and success."

Leo nodded slowly, the analogy sinking deep into his consciousness. He had always thought of control as something rigid, something forced. But the Swami's words were different. Control wasn't about force; it was about guidance, direction, and focus. It was about finding the calm in the storm, about steering through life with purpose and intention.

"The stakes are high, Leo," Swami Ananda said, his tone softening, yet no less powerful. "If you allow your mind to be governed by distractions, by the whims of the ego, you will never find true peace. You will never experience the satisfaction of a life well-lived. But if you learn to control your mind, to steer it with purpose, you will unlock a power greater than any external achievement. You will find true success—success that is not measured in money or power, but in inner peace, personal growth, and spiritual fulfillment."

Leo sat in silence, the weight of the Swami's words pressing down on him. True success. Not the success he had known in his business dealings, not the fleeting triumphs of corporate victories, but something deeper, something lasting.

"I understand," Leo said softly, though he knew that understanding was just the first step. The real challenge lay in practicing it, in learning to steer his mind with the same precision that he had once used to steer his company. But now, the stakes were far higher. His life, his peace, his very essence—these were the things he was learning to guide.

"Remember," Swami Ananda said, his voice gentle yet firm, "the mind is like the steering wheel. You must hold it with both hands, and you must steer with awareness. When you let go, when you allow distractions to pull you in every direction, you risk losing control. But when you steer with purpose, you direct your life toward the true path."

Leo took a deep breath, feeling the weight of his past decisions and future choices. He had been so caught up in the chase for external success that he had never stopped to consider the true cost of losing control over his own mind. Now, he saw it clearly—the real danger lay not in the external world, but in the internal chaos that would continue to reign unless he took the reins.

He stood up slowly, his body feeling lighter, as if something had shifted within him. "I will take control, Swami," Leo said, his voice steady. "I will steer my mind with purpose."

Swami Ananda's eyes glinted with quiet approval. "Good. The journey is long, Leo, but with each moment of awareness, you will move closer to your true self. And that, above all, is the greatest success."

Leo left the meditation hall that day with a new sense of resolve. The road ahead would not be easy. His mind would continue to pull him in different directions, and distractions would always be a part of life. But now, he had a tool—an understanding—that would help him steer through it all. And for the first time in a long while, he felt like he was moving toward something that truly mattered.

CHAPTER TWELVE

Leo stood by the window of his small room at the ashram, looking out at the distant peaks of the Himalayas, their jagged tops kissed by the golden light of dawn. The view was breathtaking, yet his mind was far from the tranquility of the scene. He was restless—restless in a way that had nothing to do with the physical surroundings. It was the pull of desire, the nagging voice in his head urging him to chase fleeting pleasures. The lure of sensory satisfaction, the comforts of his former life, tugged at him like a weight around his heart.

He had been here for weeks now, and while the stillness of the mountains had a certain peace, it also brought him face-to-face with something far more uncomfortable: his own cravings. The world he had once dominated, filled with luxury and indulgence, was now a distant memory. But the desire for those comforts still lingered in his mind, threatening to pull him back.

Swami Ananda had seen the inner turmoil Leo carried. He had observed Leo's subtle struggles with detachment. The Swami had been patient, allowing Leo time to reflect on his thoughts, to experience the full depth of his inner conflict. Now, it was time for a new lesson.

"Leo," Swami Ananda's voice broke through his reverie as he entered the room. "It is time for you to understand the true cost of desire. The pleasure-motive, the desire for sensory experiences, holds you back. It keeps you tied to the impermanent, to the fleeting."

Leo turned, meeting the Swami's gaze. "I know what you're saying, but it's harder than it sounds. I spent my whole life pursuing pleasure, seeking satisfaction in material success. Now, it feels like something is missing. I feel this constant yearning—this hunger I can't seem to satisfy."

Swami Ananda smiled gently. "This is the trap of sensory pleasures, Leo. They are like fire. They offer warmth and light in the moment, but they can also consume everything in their path. The more you chase them, the more they spread, burning everything that stands in the way."

Leo frowned, unable to deny the truth in the Swami's words. He had spent decades chasing the flames of success—the rush of new deals, the thrill of acquiring wealth, the momentary pleasures that came with power. But none of it had brought him peace. Now, the fire of desire seemed to be burning out of control within him, and he didn't know how to stop it.

Swami Ananda continued, his tone even but filled with urgency. "The key to overcoming this desire is to replace it with something greater. Meditation, self-awareness, and inner peace—these are the pursuits that will extinguish the flames of distraction. But remember, it is not enough to simply avoid the flames. You must put them out, deliberately and with purpose."

Leo blinked, trying to grasp the depth of the Swami's metaphor. "But how? How do I put out the flames of desire?"

"Imagine," the Swami began, his eyes narrowing with focus, "that your desires are like a fire—wild and consuming. It can spread quickly, overtaking everything in its path. But just as a firefighter extinguishes a blaze, you must douse your desires with the cool waters of awareness. Every time a desire rises within you, acknowledge it, understand it, but do not act on it. Allow the fire to burn itself out."

Leo absorbed the Swami's words slowly, picturing a firefighter in his mind. The firefighter did not chase the flames or run from them. Instead, he confronted them head-on, using his tools—his knowledge, his skills—to put out the fire and clear the way for safety.

"Desire is not wrong," the Swami explained, "but when it controls you, it becomes a force that drags you into chaos. It is the illusion of pleasure that keeps you enslaved. The true path to freedom is found in detachment, in replacing the fleeting pleasures with something lasting. Meditation, self-awareness, and spiritual growth—these are the fires you must cultivate, not the ones that burn you."

Leo took a deep breath, his mind swirling with the realization that his life had been driven by the desire for fleeting comforts. He had allowed the fire of desire to burn unchecked, guiding his actions, his decisions. The more he tried to satisfy one craving, the more another would arise, each one seemingly more urgent than the last.

"But it's so tempting, Swami," Leo confessed, the weight of his years of indulgence bearing down on him. "I've spent so much of my life chasing those pleasures. The rush, the satisfaction—it was all I knew. How can I let go of that now? How do I replace it with something else?"

Swami Ananda's eyes softened with understanding. "It will not be easy, Leo. The fire of desire is strong, but it is not invincible. Just as a fire burns hot in the beginning and then eventually dies down, so too will your desires. The key is to stop feeding them, to stop stoking the flames with more distractions, more indulgence. When you allow the flames to burn out, you will be left with the clarity to see that peace, true peace, comes not from the satisfaction of fleeting pleasures, but from the stillness that exists within."

Leo nodded, understanding now that the true fire to seek was one of inner peace, one that would not burn him but illuminate his path. The journey would require patience. It would require discipline. But he was ready to try. The flames of desire would no longer dictate his actions.

He stood up, feeling the weight of the lesson settle into his heart. "I will begin, Swami. I will work to extinguish the flames of desire, to clear my path and find something deeper."

Swami Ananda smiled with quiet approval. "Remember, Leo, the flames will rise again. But each time you extinguish them, you grow stronger. You become more resilient, more focused. And eventually, the fires of desire will no longer control you. You will be the one in control, guiding yourself toward a higher purpose."

Leo left the Swami's presence with a renewed sense of resolve. The flames of desire would still burn, but he now understood how to manage them. The real work would be in confronting them, acknowledging them, and choosing a different path—a path of peace, of self-awareness, of spiritual growth. And as he began this journey, he felt a glimmer of hope that the life he had been seeking all along might finally be within his reach.

CHAPTER THIRTEEN

Leo woke up early the next morning, the soft light of dawn creeping through the thin curtains of his simple ashram room. The air was still, filled only with the distant sounds of the early risers preparing for meditation. Yet despite the calm outside, Leo's mind churned with restlessness, thoughts spinning in every direction, demanding his attention. He had learned much since arriving here, but the chaos within him remained. It seemed that no matter how much he meditated or reflected, his mind remained as unruly as ever.

He thought of his days back in New York, when his mind had been his greatest ally. His sharp intellect, his ability to stay focused and make quick decisions—these were the things that had driven him to success. Yet now, as he sat in the stillness of the mountains, he realized that his mind had been far from under control. It had been ruled by external forces—desires, distractions, and an endless chase for success. Even now, though he had left behind his old life, his mind seemed incapable of settling.

It was then that Swami Ananda entered the room, as if sensing the inner turmoil Leo was experiencing.

"Leo," the Swami said with his customary calm, his voice a soothing balm to Leo's frazzled nerves. "It is time to understand something essential about the mind. It is not a simple tool that can be easily mastered. The mind is influenced by three forces, three gunas—sattva, rajas, and tamas. These are the fundamental qualities that shape the nature of your thoughts, your emotions, and your actions."

Leo looked at the Swami, intrigued but also slightly apprehensive. He had heard these words before, but their true meaning had eluded him. "What are these gunas, Swami?" he asked.

Swami Ananda smiled, his eyes twinkling with wisdom. "Sattva is the quality of purity, clarity, and balance. It is the force that brings peace, wisdom, and truth into your life. When your mind is dominated by sattva, you see the world clearly, with calm and clarity. You are in tune with your higher self and aligned with your purpose."

Leo nodded slowly, the idea of clarity and peace resonating with him. He had certainly experienced moments of such peace since arriving at the ashram, moments when his mind felt quiet and unburdened. But he knew that such moments were fleeting. "And the other two?" he asked.

"Rajas is the quality of activity, desire, and restlessness. It is the force that drives you to action, to achievement, but it also brings with it agitation, craving, and distraction. When your mind is dominated by rajas, you are constantly seeking something outside of yourself, chasing after external goals and pleasures. This quality can push you forward in life, but it also leads to frustration and anxiety if left unchecked."

Leo thought about his life in New York—the constant pressure, the endless striving, the sense of always needing more. Rajas had driven him to success, but it had also left him feeling hollow, exhausted, and unfulfilled.

"And tamas?" Leo asked, curious to understand the third guna.

"Tamas is the quality of inertia, ignorance, and darkness," Swami Ananda explained. "It is the force that leads to confusion, laziness, and despair. When your mind is dominated by tamas, you are clouded by doubt, lethargy, and a lack of direction. Tamas leads to a mind that is clouded by illusion, one that cannot see clearly or act with purpose."

Leo felt a deep sense of recognition. He had experienced all three gunas in his life, and he could clearly identify which one had dominated his thoughts and actions at different points. There were times when he had been driven by rajas, pushed by the need to prove himself, to conquer the world. But there were also moments of tamas—when his mind felt sluggish, unclear, and overwhelmed by confusion. And, though rare, there were times when he had tasted sattva, when his mind had been calm, his thoughts aligned with his true purpose.

Swami Ananda continued, "The mind is like a lens through which you perceive the world. If you look through a lens that is clouded with tamas, everything appears dark and uncertain. If you look through a lens tinted by rajas, the world becomes a place of constant desire, activity, and restlessness. But when you look through a lens of sattva, you see clearly. You perceive truth, beauty, and peace."

Leo considered the Swami's words deeply. He imagined the mind as a pair of glasses, each pair tinted by one of the three gunas. He thought of how his life had been shaped by these lenses, how the lens of rajas had driven his business ambitions, the lens of tamas had clouded his sense of purpose, and how only occasionally had he worn the lens of sattva, experiencing moments of true clarity and peace.

"How do I see through sattva more often?" Leo asked, feeling a sense of urgency rising within him. "How do I clear the lens of rajas and tamas?"

"First," Swami Ananda replied, "you must recognize when each guna is influencing your mind. When you feel restlessness or desire taking over, know that it is rajas. When you feel lethargy or confusion, know that it is tamas. And when you feel clarity, peace, and insight, you are experiencing sattva. The key is to align your actions with the qualities of sattva. This can be done through practices such as meditation, self-awareness, and mindful living. As you do this, you will gradually shift the balance of your mind toward sattva, and the influence of rajas and tamas will diminish."

Leo felt a sense of relief wash over him. This wasn't about eliminating rajas or tamas completely; it was about learning to see them for what they were and making conscious choices to cultivate sattva. It was about shifting the lens, clearing away the distractions, and choosing to view the world with a mind that was clear, balanced, and at peace.

He stood up slowly, a new sense of determination filling him. "I understand now, Swami. The mind is not just something I can control or conquer—it is something I must understand, something I must observe and shift. I will begin by observing my thoughts and actions, and by choosing to move toward sattva whenever I can."

Swami Ananda nodded, a quiet approval in his eyes. "Yes, Leo. This is the path. By understanding the nature of the mind and the influence of the three gunas, you will begin to see life more clearly, and your actions will be aligned with your higher purpose."

As Leo walked away from the Swami, he felt the weight of his past decisions lift, replaced by a newfound clarity. For the first time in a long while, he saw the path forward not as something to conquer, but as something to understand. And he knew, deep within him, that this understanding would lead him toward true peace and fulfillment.

CHAPTER FOURTEEN

Leo sat on the small wooden bench, gazing at the serene landscape of the ashram's garden. The sunlight filtered through the leaves, casting dappled shadows on the ground. It was a tranquil morning, the kind of peaceful setting he had longed for back in New York. Yet, despite the external calm, his mind was anything but still. It raced with a flurry of thoughts—about his future, about the lessons he had learned, about how much there still seemed to be to understand. The weight of it all felt overwhelming, as if the task of controlling his mind was an insurmountable challenge.

He had spent weeks at the ashram now, practicing meditation and attempting to control his thoughts. But no matter how hard he tried, his mind felt like a whirlwind, constantly shifting and tugging in every direction. Every time he thought he had gained some mastery, his thoughts would scatter again, leaving him frustrated and doubtful. Was this mind control really something he could ever achieve? Was it as difficult as it seemed?

Swami Ananda must have sensed his struggle. The Swami had been a constant, steady presence in Leo's journey, offering guidance without judgment. That morning, Leo had come to him with his frustration, explaining how the task of controlling his mind had begun to feel more like an impossible burden than a path to peace.

"Swami," Leo began, his voice tinged with frustration, "I don't know if I can do this. It feels like every time I make progress, my mind pulls me back again. I keep trying, but I don't think I'm doing it right. It's as if the harder I try, the more complicated it becomes. What am I missing?"

Swami Ananda regarded Leo with a knowing look, his eyes calm and clear. "Leo," he said softly, "the problem is not that you are trying too hard, but that you are trying to do too much. You are complicating the process. You are making it difficult."

Leo frowned. "I don't understand, Swami. I thought the point was to control the mind, to master it. Isn't it supposed to be a challenge?"

The Swami smiled gently, his expression serene. "Controlling the mind is not about making it harder than it needs to be. It is about simplicity, consistency, and patience. You must learn to approach it with ease, not force. The more you complicate the process, the more resistance you will create within yourself."

Leo paused, trying to absorb the Swami's words. "But it's so hard," he admitted. "The more I try to focus, the more my mind runs wild. It's like there's always something new demanding my attention."

The Swami nodded knowingly. "This is the nature of the mind. It is constantly in motion, constantly seeking something to latch onto. But if you approach it with force and frustration, you will only fuel the very restlessness you are trying to control. Instead, you must simplify the process."

Leo's confusion deepened. "How do I simplify it, Swami?"

"Imagine," Swami Ananda began, his voice calm and steady, "that your mind is like a desk. When you work, you need a clean and uncluttered space. If your desk is full of papers, books, and distractions, you will be unable to focus on the task at hand. Your mind is the same way. If you allow it to become cluttered with too many thoughts, worries, and desires, it will be impossible to find clarity."

Leo thought for a moment, recalling how often his desk back in New York had been piled high with papers, unfinished tasks, and ideas that never seemed to go anywhere. He remembered how, whenever he tried to focus on one task, his mind would be drawn to the chaos around him, making it hard to concentrate on anything at all.

"The key," the Swami continued, "is to keep the desk of your mind uncluttered. Instead of trying to force your mind into a state of perfect stillness, focus on removing the distractions. Clear the clutter. You don't need to make the process complicated. Simply show up every day, practice consistently, and over time, your mind will become clearer. Just as a tidy desk helps you focus, a tidy mind helps you focus."

Leo nodded slowly, the image of an uncluttered desk beginning to make sense. He had been overcomplicating his mind control practice by trying to force it to work in a way that suited his ambitious nature—by pushing himself too hard, too quickly. He had expected results without understanding the slow, steady process of cultivating focus and clarity. The more he tried to force it, the more he made it difficult.

"So," Leo asked, his voice quieter now, "what should I do to begin simplifying my practice?"

Swami Ananda's expression softened. "Start with small, consistent steps. Do not try to control every thought at once. Begin by observing your thoughts without judgment.

Let them come and go, but do not engage with them. Like cleaning a cluttered desk, you must gradually clear the space, one step at a time. Meditate for short periods, focusing on your breath or a simple mantra. Do this every day, without exception. Over time, the clutter of your mind will diminish, and your focus will become clearer."

Leo sat back, contemplating the Swami's words. It made sense—he had been trying to tackle the whole task at once, thinking he had to master it all in one go. But the mind, like any skill, required practice and patience. It was not about forcing control but about allowing the mind to settle naturally, through consistent and mindful effort.

"I understand, Swami," Leo said, feeling a sense of relief wash over him. "It's about simplicity. Not forcing it, but allowing it to happen gradually."

The Swami nodded. "Yes, Leo. The more you simplify the process, the more effective it will be. Do not overcomplicate it. Keep your mind clear, your intentions simple, and your practice steady. That is the way to success in controlling the mind."

As Leo left the Swami's presence, he felt lighter, as if a weight had been lifted from his shoulders. The task ahead no longer seemed insurmountable. By simplifying his approach, by treating his mind with the same care he would give a cluttered desk, Leo knew that he could begin to clear the distractions and focus on what truly mattered.

The road ahead would be long, but now he understood the importance of consistency, simplicity, and patience. With this new perspective, Leo felt ready to continue his journey—one small, mindful step at a time.

CHAPTER FIFTEEN

The sun hung low in the sky, casting a warm golden hue across the rugged landscape of the ashram. Leo stood at the edge of a stone path, his gaze fixed on the distant mountains. There was a certain tranquility here in the foothills of the Himalayas that he had not expected to find, but his mind remained restless. He had made progress in his quest for clarity, but the questions still lingered—was he truly understanding the path to mind control? Was he merely scratching the surface, or was there a deeper level of mastery yet to be uncovered?

It was on this day, as Leo was lost in thought, that Swami Ananda approached him with a calm yet purposeful stride. The Swami's presence was always grounding, a reminder that wisdom could be found in simplicity and patience.

"Leo," the Swami greeted, his voice gentle but firm, as if he already knew the questions swirling in Leo's mind. "You are doing well. But I sense you are still struggling with the idea of mind control. You have made progress, yet you are unsure whether you fully understand the task at hand. Am I right?"

Leo turned toward the Swami, a mixture of relief and uncertainty flooding his chest. "Yes, Swami," he admitted. "I feel like I'm getting somewhere, but I can't shake the feeling that I'm missing something. I keep thinking that mind control should be an immediate shift—a grand transformation. But maybe that's not it at all."

The Swami's eyes twinkled with understanding. "You are not alone in this, Leo. Many who first begin this journey expect a dramatic change overnight. But mind control is not about an instant transformation. It is a gradual process, one that unfolds step by step. You must understand this clearly if you wish to continue."

Leo's brows furrowed in thought. "So, it's not about forcing a change, but about a process—something that takes time?"

"Exactly," the Swami said, smiling. "Imagine that you are building a house. If you do not have a clear blueprint, the house will collapse or fail to serve its purpose. You must lay the foundation, then carefully build up from there, brick by brick. Similarly, controlling the mind is a task that requires clarity and method. It cannot be rushed, nor can it be left incomplete."

Leo felt a sudden clarity pierce through his fog of doubt. This was what he had been missing—the understanding that mind control was not an overwhelming, monumental change but a series of small, deliberate steps. He had been too focused on the outcome, too eager to master it all at once. The Swami's metaphor of building a house resonated deeply with him. It wasn't just about an end goal, but about the journey of construction, the careful planning and attention to detail that was required at each stage.

"You're saying that I need a clear plan, a blueprint for this?" Leo asked, already feeling the weight of the concept sinking in.

"Yes," Swami Ananda affirmed. "Without a clear plan, you may end up wasting energy on tasks that do not support your true goal. Just as a house is built with a plan in mind, mind control is built with understanding, patience, and persistence. You must first understand the structure of your mind, then gradually lay the foundations for control. Each day is an opportunity to reinforce that plan."

Leo stood still for a moment, absorbing the Swami's words. He thought of the times he had rushed through tasks in his business, eager for immediate results, always chasing the next deal, the next milestone. He realized now that he had approached his mind control practice with the same impatience. He had expected instant results, hoping for a miraculous shift without fully understanding the process or laying the groundwork.

"I see," Leo said slowly. "So, it's not about forcing the change all at once, but about understanding the task clearly and approaching it step by step. The clarity of the process is just as important as the goal."

The Swami nodded, his expression soft with approval. "Precisely. You must first build the mental foundation by observing your thoughts, understanding your tendencies, and then aligning your actions with your higher intentions. Only then can you move forward, layer by layer. Do not rush it, and do not be discouraged by setbacks. Like building a house, the process takes time, and each step is essential for the next."

Leo looked down at the ground, seeing the stone path that stretched out before him. Each stone was solid, stable, and placed deliberately in a row. He realized that this path was like his own journey—each small decision, each moment of mindfulness, was another stone that would help him build something lasting.

"Thank you, Swami," Leo said, feeling a deep sense of understanding settling over him. "I think I've been trying to skip steps, expecting a quick result. But now I see that this process is about steady, focused effort."

The Swami smiled gently. "That is the key, Leo. Mind control is not a task that can be completed overnight. It is a lifelong process of building, one thought at a time. Keep your blueprint in mind, and each day, take small, consistent steps forward. You will build something strong and lasting, just as a house is built with intention and care."

Leo felt a surge of gratitude and clarity. The task ahead no longer seemed daunting or impossible. With the understanding that mind control was a gradual process, he could approach it with patience and a clear sense of direction. Each small step, each moment of mindfulness, would build toward the lasting change he sought.

As he walked away from the Swami, Leo felt a newfound sense of calm. He had a plan now, a blueprint for his mind, and he was ready to begin constructing it—one steady step at a time.

CHAPTER SIXTEEN

The air in the ashram was thick with the scent of earth and blooming flowers, the morning sun casting long shadows across the lush garden. Leo had begun to appreciate these quiet moments of stillness more than ever. There was something about the simple beauty of nature that grounded him, something he had long been disconnected from in his former life in New York. Yet, despite the outer peace of the environment, Leo knew that the true challenge lay within. How could he cultivate that same sense of peace in his mind?

For the past several weeks, Leo had been diligently practicing meditation, following Swami Ananda's guidance. But even now, as he sat cross-legged in the garden, the steady hum of thoughts continued to buzz around him, a chaotic inner noise that seemed to always lurk in the background. He could no longer ignore it. He had to understand the root of this inner turbulence, this constant mental restlessness.

It was on this particular morning, as Leo was pondering these thoughts, that Swami Ananda appeared at his side, walking with his characteristic quiet grace. The Swami smiled gently at Leo before sitting beside him, his eyes sparkling with a wisdom that Leo had come to trust.

"Leo," Swami Ananda said, his voice a soft melody in the quiet of the garden. "You've made progress, but I sense you are still struggling to cultivate true inner peace. The garden outside you is beautiful, but your inner landscape is still wild and unruly. Do you understand why?"

Leo turned to look at him, feeling a flicker of recognition. "Yes, Swami. I've been meditating and trying to control my thoughts, but they keep rushing back. I feel like I haven't been able to create the right environment inside of me for peace to grow. My mind feels like an untended garden—overgrown, chaotic."

Swami Ananda nodded, his expression calm but knowing. "The mind is much like a garden, Leo. If you wish to cultivate peace, you must first create a favourable environment—an environment that allows positive thoughts to flourish and negative ones to wither away. This is not something that happens by force. You must tend to your inner climate with care, just as a gardener tends to a garden."

Leo listened intently, trying to absorb the Swami's words. "So, it's not just about controlling the thoughts. It's about creating the right conditions for positive thoughts to grow, right?"

"Exactly," the Swami affirmed. "A garden needs the right amount of sunlight, water, and soil to thrive. Similarly, your mind needs positivity, discipline, and detachment in order to cultivate peace. If the soil of your mind is filled with negative emotions, distractions, and desires, it will be difficult for any positive thoughts to take root."

Leo sat still for a moment, visualizing the image of a garden. He could almost see it—his mind as a garden, each thought a seed. Some seeds grew into beautiful flowers, while others turned into weeds that choked the life out of the good ones. He had spent so much time trying to forcefully pluck out the weeds, not realizing that the key was to focus on nurturing the positive plants, creating an environment where they could thrive.

"I see now," Leo said slowly. "It's not enough to just remove the weeds. I have to create a space where good thoughts can grow on their own."

The Swami's smile widened, his eyes gleaming with approval. "That is the essence of cultivating the mind. You do not need to fight against the weeds of negative thoughts all the time. Instead, focus on nurturing the good thoughts. The more you nourish positivity, discipline, and detachment, the less space there will be for the negative to take root. When your inner climate is favorable, peace will naturally blossom."

Leo thought for a moment, remembering his busy, high-pressure life in New York. He had always been caught up in the rush—hustling from one task to another, one deal to the next, never taking the time to create a peaceful inner environment. His mind had been filled with the weeds of stress, anxiety, and greed, while the seeds of contentment, balance, and mindfulness had been buried beneath the chaos. No wonder he felt so lost and empty despite his outward success.

"But how do I begin creating this favorable environment?" Leo asked, his voice earnest. "How do I tend to the garden of my mind?"

The Swami's gaze softened, and he placed a gentle hand on Leo's shoulder. "Start with small, deliberate actions, Leo. Just as a gardener must begin with one seed, you must begin with one thought. Focus on cultivating discipline in your daily practices—your meditation, your work, your relationships. Make space for detachment, for letting go of things that do not serve you. Allow only positive thoughts to take root. Avoid the distractions that feed negativity.

When you nurture discipline, detachment, and positivity, your mind will begin to clear, and peace will take root. Remember, just as a garden needs patience, so too does the mind."

Leo closed his eyes for a moment, letting the Swami's words sink in. He visualized his mind as a garden—calm, balanced, with room for growth. Each positive thought was like a blooming flower, filling the space with color and light. He realized that his focus had always been on external achievements, but the true work began within.

"Thank you, Swami," Leo said, his heart lighter now, a sense of direction settling within him. "I will start by creating the right conditions, by nurturing my mind with discipline and positivity."

The Swami nodded, his smile warm and wise. "Remember, Leo, that a garden requires ongoing care. It is not enough to plant the seeds and walk away. You must tend to it every day, with patience and love. In time, your mind will reflect the peace you cultivate within it."

As Leo walked through the garden, he felt a new sense of responsibility—not just toward the work ahead of him but toward the work within. His mind, like a garden, could flourish in peace if he tended it properly. He knew now that the task of controlling his mind was not one of force or struggle, but of creating the right inner climate, a climate that would allow positivity to grow and negativity to fade away.

With this new understanding, Leo felt a deep sense of resolve. The work was long-term, but the process had begun. The garden of his mind was ready for cultivation, and he was ready to begin.

CHAPTER SEVENTEEN

The wind howled through the trees as Leo stood on the balcony of the small guesthouse in the hills, looking out over the valley below. The view was breathtaking, but his mind was far from calm. It had been a few weeks since he arrived in India, and he had made some progress with his meditation and the teachings of Swami Ananda, but there were still moments—moments of intense stress and emotion—where his mind seemed to slip away from him.

He had heard the Swami speak many times about the importance of discipline and control. But now, as he faced the deepening turbulence in his thoughts, Leo realized that the real challenge lay in knowing how to manage the mind, not just in moments of stillness, but also in times of crisis, when the world around him seemed to close in.

Just as he was lost in thought, he heard the familiar, calming footsteps of Swami Ananda approach. The Swami stepped beside Leo, his presence quiet yet all-encompassing, like a steady breeze.

"Leo," the Swami said, his voice both gentle and knowing, "I see that your mind is restless. What troubles you?"

Leo sighed deeply, feeling the weight of the question. "I thought I had made progress, Swami. But I'm finding that when I'm under pressure, when things start to go wrong or when the weight of the world feels heavy, I lose control. I can't seem to stay calm in those moments."

Swami Ananda nodded, as if expecting this admission. "This is a natural part of the journey, Leo. Even the most disciplined minds can falter under stress. It is not enough to practice discipline only in moments of peace. You must learn to be equipped with inner tools, not only for regular use, but also for the moments when stress and chaos arise."

Leo looked at him, intrigued. "Tools? What do you mean?"

"Just as a craftsman keeps a toolbox filled with tools for different tasks," the Swami explained, "you must have two sets of inner disciplines: one for your regular practice, and another for times of crisis. Both are necessary, but each serves a different purpose."

Leo's brow furrowed as he tried to understand. "So, one set of disciplines is for the everyday practice of meditation and mindfulness, and the other is for those urgent moments when I feel overwhelmed? But how do I prepare for those moments? I can't predict them."

Swami Ananda smiled, his eyes twinkling with understanding. "Exactly. You cannot predict the crises that will arise, but you can prepare yourself for them. Think of it as a toolbox. Just as you would have a wrench, a hammer, and a screwdriver for various tasks, you must have specific practices at your disposal for both daily peace and moments of chaos. When stress hits, you will need tools that will immediately ground you, bringing you back to a place of calm."

Leo nodded slowly, beginning to understand. "So, the regular practices—like meditation and reflection—build my foundation. But the emergency measures are for when I'm in the middle of a storm, when everything seems out of control."

"Precisely," Swami Ananda affirmed. "For your regular discipline, you need practices that anchor you and help you create the right mental climate. Meditation, mindfulness, and observing your thoughts regularly build a foundation of inner peace. But when you face sudden stress, there must be a set of emergency measures—quick, effective practices that you can use to bring your mind back to balance immediately. Think of these as your 'mental first aid kit.'"

Leo felt a sense of clarity begin to form. "So, in moments of intense pressure, I don't have time to sit down for a long meditation session. I need something immediate—something that will work in the heat of the moment."

"Exactly," the Swami said, his voice soft yet firm. "For example, deep breathing can be an emergency measure. It is quick and effective, calming the mind almost instantly. Another tool could be focusing on a mantra or a positive affirmation—something simple to redirect your thoughts. Detaching yourself from the situation by observing it from a distance is also a powerful tool. The key is not to wait until the crisis occurs to start practicing these measures. Like a craftsman, you must practice using your tools regularly, so that they are sharp and effective when you need them most."

Leo felt a sense of relief at the simplicity of the Swami's advice. "I can start practicing these emergency tools regularly, so I'm not caught off guard when stress hits."

"Exactly," the Swami said, "And you must also remember that inner discipline is not just about the tools you use. It's also about the intention behind their use. When you are under stress, do not approach your tools with resistance or frustration. Use them with patience and compassion, just as a gardener tends to plants with care."

Leo's thoughts drifted back to his time in New York, to the countless moments when stress had taken over, when he had felt powerless and out of control. It seemed so clear to him now—he had never thought of managing his mind as a toolbox. He had tried to force calmness, to push away the chaos, but now he saw that it was about equipping himself with the right tools and practices that could bring him back to center.

"I see," Leo said, feeling a surge of determination. "So, I need to not only have regular practices to build discipline, but also a set of emergency tools that will help me in moments of crisis. Both sets are equally important."

The Swami nodded approvingly. "Indeed. The daily practices build your resilience, while the emergency tools provide immediate relief when needed. Both work together to create a balanced, controlled mind."

Leo felt a sense of peace settle within him. The idea of having a toolbox, a set of reliable practices to rely on, made the task of mind control seem much more manageable. He could start small, adding tools to his mental kit, using them regularly, and knowing that when the storms of life hit, he would be prepared.

"Thank you, Swami," Leo said, his voice filled with gratitude. "This makes so much sense. I now have a clear approach—practicing daily and equipping myself for those unexpected moments of stress."

Swami Ananda smiled, his eyes warm with understanding. "Remember, Leo, the mind is like a garden. Tend to it daily, but also be prepared for the unexpected storms. With the right tools, you can weather any storm, and continue to grow."

Leo walked back into the ashram with a renewed sense of purpose. He knew the journey ahead would require patience and consistency, but now he had a clear understanding of how to approach it—building his mental toolbox one tool at a time, ready for whatever life would throw his way.

CHAPTER EIGHTEEN

The air was thick with the scent of incense, a light mist curling through the courtyard as Leo sat quietly beside the serene lotus pond in the center of the ashram. His gaze followed the ripples on the water, disturbed only by the occasional breeze. He felt a strange sense of stillness inside, a quietness that had eluded him for most of his life. He had spent so many years chasing success, power, and external validation that he had failed to notice the turbulence within his own mind. But now, as he sat in silence, he began to understand something fundamental—something that had been missing from his life.

Swami Ananda approached, his footsteps soft on the stone path. Leo turned to face him, noting the familiar sense of calm that seemed to emanate from the Swami like a gentle wave.

"You look peaceful today, Leo," the Swami remarked, his voice light but perceptive. "What is it that you are contemplating?"

Leo smiled, feeling the truth of his own thoughts settling into place. "I was just thinking about the nature of the mind. It's strange, Swami. I feel more at peace than I have in years, yet the world around me remains as chaotic as ever. Why is it that when the mind is pure, it feels so much easier to control?"

Swami Ananda sat beside him, folding his legs into a meditative posture. "That is the essence of true mind control, Leo. The clearer the mind, the easier it is to master. A pure mind, free of negative emotions, attachments, and distractions, is like clear water—it allows for effortless reflection and control."

Leo leaned back, reflecting on the Swami's words. He could see it now, how his mind had often been clouded with negative emotions—anger, fear, and desire. It had been like trying to navigate a boat through murky waters. Every thought, every decision had been clouded by these emotions, making it difficult to see clearly and control his reactions.

"Clear water..." Leo repeated, as if savoring the imagery. "That's what it is, isn't it? A pure mind is like clear water. It doesn't resist. It flows. It reflects."

"Yes," the Swami said, his eyes glinting with quiet wisdom. "When your mind is pure, it becomes a mirror of your true self. Your thoughts no longer cloud your perception. Just like clear water allows you to see the bottom of a pond, a pure mind allows you to see the truth of your situation, of your thoughts, and of your actions. In such a mind, control comes naturally."

Leo thought back to the early days of his journey—his constant striving, his battles with his own desires, and his frantic search for external success. His mind had always been turbulent, a whirlpool of thoughts and emotions that kept him from seeing clearly. Now, in the stillness of the ashram, he realized how much of his restlessness had stemmed from his own mental impurities.

"What are the impurities in the mind, Swami?" Leo asked, his curiosity deepening. "And how do I remove them?"

The Swami smiled gently, his voice calm. "The mind is clouded by three primary impurities, Leo—attachment, aversion, and ignorance. Attachment binds you to things, people, and desires, causing you to cling to them in a way that disturbs your inner peace. Aversion creates resistance to things you do not like, leading to frustration, anger, and negative emotions. Ignorance is the greatest impurity—it is the lack of awareness of your true nature, the belief that you are separate from the world and from your higher self."

Leo absorbed the Swami's words, realizing how each impurity had shaped his thoughts and decisions over the years. He had been attached to wealth and success, constantly striving for more, never content with what he had. He had harbored aversions—toward his failures, his critics, his insecurities—and those had fueled his anger and fear. But most of all, he had lived in ignorance, unaware of the deeper truths of life, of the nature of his mind, and of the possibility of inner peace.

"So, to purify the mind, I must release attachments, overcome aversions, and dispel ignorance?" Leo asked.

"Yes," the Swami replied. "But the process is not about fighting these impurities. It is about cultivating the opposite qualities—detachment, acceptance, and awareness. Detachment allows you to let go of what binds you. Acceptance allows you to embrace life as it is, without resistance. Awareness brings clarity, helping you see your true nature and the interconnectedness of all things."

Leo nodded slowly, as if each word was sinking deeper into his consciousness. He had spent so much of his life fighting against life, trying to control it, trying to force things to go his way. Now, for the first time, he understood that control was not about resistance; it was about understanding, acceptance, and clarity.

"You have already begun the process, Leo," the Swami continued. "Through your meditation and mindfulness, you are clearing the clouds of the mind. With each practice, the water becomes clearer, and the reflections become sharper. In time, the impurities will dissolve, and the mind will become naturally pure, like the stillest lake."

Leo took a deep breath, feeling a sense of peace wash over him. He thought back to his life in New York, to the countless times he had been driven by fear and desire. He saw now how much energy he had wasted on clinging to things and resisting what was. The true path to control, he realized, was not to force the mind into submission but to purify it, to clear away the clouds and allow the natural flow of peace and clarity to take over.

"I understand, Swami," Leo said quietly. "The purer the mind, the easier it is to control. It's not about forcing things. It's about clearing the mind, letting go of the impurities, and allowing the true nature of the mind to emerge."

"Exactly," the Swami replied with a serene smile. "A pure mind is like clear water—it reflects the world as it is and allows you to navigate it with ease and grace. As you continue to purify your mind, you will find that control comes naturally, without effort."

Leo closed his eyes, feeling the stillness within him deepen. He visualized his mind as a calm, clear lake, its surface smooth and unruffled. As he sat there, surrounded by the beauty of the ashram, he knew that the journey ahead was one of constant cultivation—not of external achievements, but of inner clarity and peace.

In the purity of his mind, Leo realized, there was no need for struggle. There was only the clear reflection of truth, and in that reflection, control came effortlessly.

CHAPTER NINETEEN

The sun was just beginning to set over the distant mountains, casting long shadows across the meditation hall where Leo sat in quiet contemplation. The Swami had told him that true mastery of the mind came not from forcing control over it, but from changing its very constitution. Leo had heard this phrase many times before, but today, the weight of it settled deeply within him. He was beginning to understand that his mind, with its constant turmoil, its restless desires, and its patterns of reaction, could be transformed—just as an alchemist could turn base metal into gold.

Swami Ananda entered the hall, his presence calm and centered, like a still rock in the midst of a raging river. He sat beside Leo, observing the silence for a moment before speaking.

"Leo," the Swami began, his voice soft, yet imbued with a quiet power, "I have seen your efforts in purifying your mind. But now, I want to speak of something deeper—the transformation of the very constitution of the mind. Just as an alchemist changes base metal into gold, so too can you change the makeup of your mind. This change is not instant; it is gradual, but it is powerful."

Leo turned to face the Swami, a spark of curiosity igniting within him. "You've spoken of purifying the mind, but now you're talking about changing its very nature.

What does that mean exactly, Swami?"

The Swami smiled, nodding gently. "The mind, by nature, is composed of three gunas—sattva, rajas, and tamas. These three qualities determine how the mind operates. Sattva is purity, clarity, and calmness. Rajas is the quality of activity, desire, and restlessness. Tamas is inertia, ignorance, and confusion. In most minds, these three qualities are in constant fluctuation, but the key to mastery lies in increasing sattva, the purity, to dominate the other two."

Leo absorbed the Swami's words slowly, his mind racing with understanding. "So, if I increase sattva, I can create a mind that is more calm and focused, less driven by desires and distractions?"

"Exactly," the Swami replied. "When sattva is increased, the mind becomes clearer, steadier, and more in tune with higher truths. Rajas, the restless desire for achievement, will calm. Tamas, the inertia that keeps you stuck in ignorance and confusion, will dissolve. In time, with consistent effort, you can change the very constitution of your mind."

Leo reflected on his life in New York, on the constant craving for more—more success, more wealth, more recognition. That restlessness, that drive, had once fueled him, but now it felt empty. The deeper he delved into the Swami's teachings, the more he realized that this relentless desire was a product of his own mind, governed by rajas. He needed to replace that with something more enduring.

"But how do I increase sattva?" Leo asked. "How do I change the very fabric of my mind?"

Swami Ananda closed his eyes for a moment, as if summoning ancient wisdom. "To increase sattva, Leo, you must begin with your actions and thoughts. Purify what you consume—both physically and mentally. Just as the body is nourished by food, the mind is nourished by thoughts, emotions, and experiences. By practicing virtues such as truth, compassion, humility, and equanimity, you feed the mind with pure energy. Meditate regularly, cultivate awareness, and detach from worldly desires. The more you practice, the more sattva will arise naturally."

Leo nodded, a sense of understanding washing over him. It was clear now. His restless mind had been nurtured by his constant pursuit of external desires. But by redirecting his energy toward purity, toward virtuous living, he could transform that very nature. He could, in essence, be his own alchemist.

The Swami continued, his voice rich with meaning. "In the beginning, it will feel as though your efforts are small, like a single grain of gold in a vast sea of lead. But remember, the alchemist does not work with haste. He understands that transformation takes time. Every virtuous thought, every moment of stillness, adds a little more sattva to the mind. With practice, you will notice a change. The desires will lessen. The distractions will fade. The mind will begin to reflect the calmness of the purest gold."

Leo thought of the many distractions he had once chased—richer deals, faster success, more power. It had always felt like a never-ending pursuit, one that left him constantly dissatisfied. Now, for the first time, he understood that this pursuit was not the answer. The key to true fulfillment lay in the alchemy of the mind.

"So, changing the constitution of the mind is about purifying the mind's substances—its thoughts, desires, and actions—until they align with sattva?" Leo asked.

"Yes," Swami Ananda affirmed. "And in this process, the mind becomes like the finest gold—free from impurities, calm, and able to reflect the highest truths. The more you increase sattva, the more effortless it becomes to control the mind. It is like the alchemist, who, with patience and skill, transforms base metal into something of immeasurable value. The mind, when purified and composed of sattva, becomes the greatest treasure you can possess."

Leo sat in silence, the Swami's words echoing through him. For so long, he had searched for external treasures, for wealth and power. But now, he realized that the greatest treasure was already within him—his own mind, capable of transformation, capable of becoming pure gold.

He closed his eyes, imagining the process of purification, of alchemy. With each deep breath, he envisioned his mind becoming lighter, clearer, more refined. The distractions, the desires, and the frustrations faded away like impurities being washed from the surface of gold. In their place, a sense of peace, clarity, and control emerged.

"I see it now," Leo said softly, his voice filled with resolve. "The mind is like base metal, full of distractions and desires. But with patience, with consistency, and with the right practices, I can transform it into something pure, something valuable—like gold."

Swami Ananda's smile was gentle, but there was a depth of wisdom in it. "Yes, Leo. The alchemy of the mind is the most powerful transformation you can undergo. And as you change your mind, you change your life. With a pure mind, all things are possible."

Leo opened his eyes and looked out across the mountains, the fading light of the sun painting the sky with hues of gold and pink. The journey ahead was long, but for the first time, he felt a deep sense of peace. He was no longer chasing after fleeting desires. He was embarking on a journey of inner transformation, one that would bring him the true peace and control he had always sought.

And like the alchemist turning base metal into gold, Leo knew that he, too, could transform the very constitution of his mind.

CHAPTER TWENTY

The early morning sun streamed through the trees as Leo sat in the serene courtyard of the ashram. The air was cool, tinged with the earthy scent of dew on the grass. For weeks now, he had been immersing himself in the teachings of Swami Ananda, struggling through the mental turmoil of his past life and the slow process of transformation. But today, something felt different. There was a peace here, in the quiet company of the Swami and his disciples, that Leo had not experienced in years.

As he sat cross-legged, his eyes half-closed in meditation, Leo thought about the times when his mind had been at its most scattered, when he had sought fulfillment in the fleeting pleasures of the world. There had been no peace in the constant chase for more—more wealth, more success, more validation. Now, surrounded by people who seemed content with the present moment, who lived by a sense of purpose and discipline, Leo felt a subtle but powerful shift inside.

Swami Ananda entered the courtyard, his presence as calming as ever. He walked slowly, as if each step was measured in timeless wisdom. His disciples followed, their faces serene, embodying the peace that Leo longed to achieve.

"Leo," Swami Ananda said, his voice gentle yet firm, "today, we will talk about the power of holy company in the process of mind control."

Leo looked up, curious. "Holy company?" he repeated. "How does being around others help control the mind?"

The Swami sat beside him, folding his hands in his lap. "You see, Leo, the mind is influenced by the company it keeps. Just as the body is nourished by food, the mind is nourished by its surroundings—by the people it associates with, the ideas it absorbs, and the energies it encounters. When you are surrounded by spiritually advanced individuals, those whose minds are disciplined and whose actions are aligned with higher principles, their presence has a profound effect on your own mind. They set a positive example and offer a kind of subtle guidance that helps you stay on track."

Leo's brow furrowed. "But how exactly does this work? Isn't mind control something I must do alone, through my own effort?"

"Ah," the Swami smiled, his eyes twinkling with understanding. "It is true that mind control requires individual effort. But just as a lamp cannot shine in the darkness without being lit, a person cannot progress alone without the light of good company. When you are surrounded by individuals who radiate calm, focus, and clarity, their light will inevitably illuminate your own path. Their presence can dispel the darkness of confusion and restlessness within you."

Leo thought back to his life in New York, to the people he had spent his time with—the businessmen driven by ambition, the endless network of contacts who cared more about deals than personal growth. They had shaped his mind, but in a way that had kept him restless and unsatisfied. What would it have been like to be surrounded by those who lived with purpose, whose thoughts were aligned with higher goals?

The Swami continued, "Think of holy company as a lamp sharing its light. When you sit near a lamp, its light spreads, illuminating everything around it. Similarly, when you spend time in the company of those who have cultivated inner peace and self-discipline, their light spreads to you, offering clarity and helping you navigate the distractions of the mind. Good company acts as a guide, pointing you in the right direction."

Leo nodded slowly. He had seen it in the Swami and his disciples. Their calmness, their poise—it wasn't just an act; it was a reflection of their inner discipline. They lived by the same principles that Leo had been struggling to understand. They were the light, and by simply being in their presence, Leo felt as though his mind could relax, even if just for a moment.

"I've noticed it," Leo said, looking out over the peaceful landscape. "When I'm with you, with all of you, it's like my mind slows down. It feels lighter, less burdened."

"Exactly," the Swami said, a knowing smile on his face. "This is the power of holy company. It's not just about being around people—it's about being around people who inspire you to grow, who challenge you to be better, and who embody the very qualities you wish to cultivate in yourself."

Leo sat back, taking it all in. The city he had come from had been a world of noise and ambition, a place where people were constantly rushing to get ahead. Here, in this ashram, surrounded by people whose lives were guided by inner peace and purpose, Leo felt a deep sense of calm. It was as though the very air in the ashram was different, filled with a subtle energy that helped him stay focused and grounded.

"I've always thought that to control my mind, I had to do it alone," Leo said, more to himself than to the Swami. "But now I see that the right company, the right environment, can make a huge difference."

Swami Ananda nodded. "Indeed, Leo. We are social creatures by nature. The environment we immerse ourselves in influences our thoughts, actions, and attitudes. That's why it is said that a person is known by the company they keep. By seeking the company of those who walk the path of wisdom and peace, you will begin to walk that path yourself. Their light will guide you, just as you will, in turn, share your light with others."

Leo felt a sense of deep gratitude well up inside him. It wasn't just the teachings or the meditation that was helping him—it was the people around him. The calm presence of the Swami, the silent discipline of the disciples, the shared commitment to growth. All of it was having an impact on him, whether he realized it or not.

Looking up at the Swami, Leo asked, "How can I find more of this company when I return to the world?"

The Swami's eyes softened. "Seek those who seek truth, Leo. Seek those who are not driven by worldly desires, but by a deeper purpose. It may not always be easy to find such company, but when you do, hold onto it. Surround yourself with those who help you rise higher, not those who pull you back into the distractions of the world."

Leo nodded, feeling a renewed sense of determination. For so long, he had felt trapped by his own desires and the people around him. But now, he understood that the key to true mind control wasn't just about internal discipline—it was about the company he kept. The people who surrounded him would either help him grow or keep him stagnant.

As he sat there, the light of the setting sun casting a golden glow over the courtyard, Leo made a silent promise to himself. He would seek out the company of those who embodied the qualities he desired—peace, wisdom, and inner strength. He would walk with those whose light could guide him on his journey, and in doing so, he would cultivate the same light within himself.

Just as the lamp spreads its light, Leo knew that in the company of those who radiated peace, he, too, would find his way to clarity, control, and inner freedom.

The sun had risen high in the sky, its golden rays illuminating the peaceful grounds of the ashram. Leo sat beneath a large banyan tree, his eyes closed as he focused on his breath. The morning was still, and the only sound that filled the air was the occasional rustle of leaves in the gentle breeze. It had been a few weeks since Leo had made the decision to stay longer at the ashram, and during this time, he had been learning to practice self-discipline, meditation, and focus. But the Swami's teachings had introduced him to a deeper concept, one that he was now eager to understand.

Leo had come to learn about the three gunas—sattva, rajas, and tamas—the qualities that influence the mind and actions of all living beings. Sattva, the quality of purity, harmony, and balance, was the one that Leo longed to cultivate. But there was something about it that eluded him, something that made his efforts seem insufficient. Despite his discipline, his mind still wandered. It was as though the purity he sought was always just out of reach.

Swami Ananda arrived, as always, with a quiet grace. His presence felt like a balm to Leo's restless thoughts. Today, the Swami seemed to have something important to share.

"Leo," he said softly, taking a seat beside him. "Today, I will explain how sattva is purified. It is essential to understand that sattva, though a natural quality of the mind, requires purification through constant effort and the right practices."

Leo listened attentively, eager for the answer to the lingering questions in his mind. "How is sattva purified, Swami?" he asked.

The Swami smiled, his eyes reflecting the depth of his wisdom. "Sattva is purified in three essential ways: through good company, ethical living, and spiritual practices."

Leo nodded thoughtfully. He could understand the idea of good company, having felt the transformative power of the Swami's presence and the peaceful influence of the other disciples. But the other two aspects—ethical living and spiritual practices—needed further explanation.

"Let me explain," the Swami continued, his voice calm yet authoritative. "Good company, or *satsanga*, is the first and most important means of purifying sattva. When you surround yourself with individuals who embody purity of thought, speech, and action, their presence acts as a filter, removing impurities from your own mind. Just as you cannot expect to keep a pond clean if the water around it is polluted, you cannot purify your mind if you remain in the company of those who nourish negative tendencies."

Leo had already experienced the impact of good company. The calm and discipline of those around him had made it easier to quiet his restless thoughts. But the Swami's words made him realize that this process was not just about being near the right people—it was about absorbing their qualities, their mindset, and allowing those qualities to purify his own mind.

The Swami paused, allowing Leo to digest his words. "The second means of purifying sattva is through ethical living. Sattva is nurtured when you live according to principles of truth, non-violence, compassion, and integrity. Your actions should align with your higher purpose, and your heart should be free from malice, greed, and selfish desires. When your life is guided by these ethical principles, your mind becomes clearer and purer, and you will find that sattva naturally increases."

Leo reflected on his own life, the many compromises he had made in the name of success, the times when his actions had been guided more by ambition than by integrity. He could see now that true purity of mind was not just about controlling his thoughts, but also about purifying his actions—ensuring they were aligned with his deeper values.

Finally, the Swami spoke of spiritual practices. "The third means of purifying sattva is through regular spiritual practices. Meditation, prayer, mindfulness, and contemplation help you connect to your higher self and clear the mental fog. Through consistent practice, you begin to calm the mind, strengthen willpower, and align your thoughts with divine wisdom. Spiritual practices purify the mind the way a filter purifies water—removing impurities and leaving only clarity and purity behind."

Leo could already see the effects of meditation and mindfulness in his own life. The chaos of his thoughts had begun to subside, and moments of clarity—though still fleeting—had started to appear with greater frequency. The Swami's teachings about purification made him realize that his mental discipline had to be accompanied by a more profound ethical and spiritual commitment.

"Sattva," the Swami concluded, "is not something you can purify overnight. It requires patience, consistency, and the right environment. Just as water is purified by filtering it through layers of sand and charcoal, sattva is purified through good company, ethical living, and spiritual practices."

Leo sat in silence for a moment, absorbing the depth of the Swami's words. It was a lot to take in, but it made sense. Sattva was not something that could be attained passively—it had to be nurtured and cultivated with intention.

He thought back to his life in New York, to the countless decisions he had made based on ambition and short-term desires. He had sought success in the wrong places, chasing after material gain and status, neglecting the inner work that would have brought him true fulfillment.

Now, here in the ashram, surrounded by the teachings of the Swami and the example of the disciples, Leo began to understand that the real work was not just about controlling his mind—it was about purifying it, aligning it with higher values, and cultivating the qualities that would lead him to peace and fulfillment.

The Swami smiled at him, as if sensing his inner shift. "Remember, Leo, the mind is like a river. If you let it flow aimlessly, it becomes muddy and polluted. But if you direct it and purify it, the waters become clear, and the flow becomes steady. Purify your mind with good company, ethical living, and spiritual practices, and you will find that sattva becomes your natural state."

Leo nodded, a new sense of determination rising within him. He was beginning to understand the process of purification, and with each lesson, he could feel himself moving closer to the peace and clarity he had long sought. It was a journey, a long one, but he knew now that he was on the right path. Just as a filter clears water, his commitment to these practices would gradually purify his mind, making it clear, steady, and aligned with his higher purpose.

CHAPTER TWENTY-TWO

The morning mist lingered in the air as Leo stood at the edge of the ashram's open courtyard, gazing out at the distant mountains. The stillness was broken only by the gentle sound of birds chirping, and the soft rustle of leaves in the wind. In the early hours of the day, the Swami had invited Leo to join him in practicing yoga, a tradition that had become a cornerstone of the daily routine at the ashram. Today, Leo felt a sense of anticipation as he stepped onto the well-worn yoga mat, ready to learn more about the connection between yoga and mind control.

Swami Ananda appeared beside him, calm as ever. "Leo," he began, his voice steady, "today we will learn about the basic yoga disciplines that are essential for controlling the mind."

Leo stood quietly, eager to absorb every word. He had practiced yoga before, mostly in passing, but it was always more for physical health than spiritual growth. However, the Swami's teachings had already helped him to see the connection between mind and body, and he knew that yoga, in its true form, was a powerful tool for the work he needed to do on himself.

"Yoga," the Swami continued, "is more than just a physical exercise. It is a practice that brings harmony to the body, mind, and soul. The goal of yoga is to quiet the mind, create mental clarity, and bring one closer to a higher state of awareness. There are three key disciplines in yoga that help achieve mind control: *asanas* (physical postures), *pranayama* (breath control), and *dhyana* (meditation)."

Leo listened intently, already familiar with the first discipline—*asanas*. They were the physical postures, the movements that stretched and strengthened the body. But he had never considered how these movements could be linked to mind control.

"The first discipline," the Swami said, "is asanas. These physical postures are not just about flexibility or strength. They are designed to bring stability to the body, allowing the energy to flow freely and promoting mental clarity. When the body is aligned and relaxed, the mind follows suit. The discipline of asanas prepares you for deeper practices like pranayama and dhyana."

As the Swami demonstrated, Leo carefully followed along. The stretches and poses seemed simple at first, but each movement required focus and attention. Leo felt the tension in his muscles, but he also noticed that with each deep breath, the mental chatter in his mind began to fade. His body was no longer just an instrument of movement—it was a gateway to stillness.

"The second discipline," the Swami continued, "is pranayama, or breath control. The breath is the bridge between the body and the mind. When you control the breath, you control the mind. Pranayama helps regulate the energy in the body, calming the nervous system and calming the restless mind."

The Swami guided Leo through several pranayama techniques—alternate nostril breathing, deep belly breathing, and the powerful *kapalbhati*, or breath of fire. Leo felt a noticeable shift in his energy as he focused on his breath. The mental fog, the endless stream of thoughts that had plagued him for so long, began to clear. Each inhale brought a sense of calm, and each exhale carried away tension and restlessness. Leo had never realized how deeply connected the breath was to his mental state.

"With pranayama," the Swami said, "you can steady the mind and prepare it for the final discipline—dhyana, or meditation. Meditation is the highest form of mind control. It allows you to reach the deepest states of stillness, where the mind is no longer caught up in the turbulence of thoughts and emotions. In meditation, you can experience a state of pure awareness, free from the distractions of the world."

Leo nodded, understanding now how the practices of asanas and pranayama were laying the foundation for what would come next. The mind, he realized, was not an entity that could be controlled through sheer force. It was a tool that needed to be nurtured, guided, and prepared through physical discipline and breath control.

The Swami continued, "Think of these disciplines like the yoga mat beneath you. Just as the mat provides a stable foundation for your practice, these disciplines provide a stable foundation for your mind. Without them, the mind is like a wild horse—difficult to tame and unpredictable. But when you practice these disciplines consistently, you will find that the mind becomes steady, like a well-trained horse."

Leo thought about the yoga mat beneath his feet, its surface providing the grip and support needed for each pose. The analogy made sense. Yoga was more than a set of movements—it was the foundation for building the inner strength required to control the mind.

As the session came to a close, Leo felt a quiet sense of accomplishment. His body was sore from the new movements, but his mind was clearer than it had been in years. The chaotic thoughts that had once clouded his judgment now seemed distant, as if they were slowly being replaced with calm and clarity.

The Swami smiled at Leo, sensing the shift in his awareness. "Remember," he said, "the practices of yoga are not meant to be mastered in a single day. They are lifelong disciplines, and their effects will grow stronger the more you commit to them. Just as a yoga mat supports your practice, these disciplines will support your journey toward mind control."

Leo stood, feeling the ground beneath him solidify in a way it never had before. He had learned something profound today—not just about yoga, but about the nature of the mind itself. Each discipline, each practice, was a step toward mastery—not just of the body, but of the mind. And as he rolled up his yoga mat, Leo knew that this journey was only just beginning.

CHAPTER TWENTY-THREE

The sun had begun its descent, casting long shadows across the serene ashram grounds. Leo had spent the day in quiet reflection, contemplating the Swami's latest lesson on the practice of discrimination, or *viveka*. This concept was a cornerstone of the spiritual journey, and Leo could feel its significance sinking deeper into his understanding with each passing day.

Swami Ananda had explained to him earlier that the essence of *viveka* lay in the ability to distinguish between the eternal and the non-eternal, between what truly matters and what is fleeting. It was a subtle practice, one that required not just intellectual clarity but deep awareness—a skill that Leo had to cultivate if he wished to free his mind from the constant clutter of desires, distractions, and illusions.

As evening settled in, Leo met the Swami in the courtyard, where they often sat and discussed the day's lessons. The calm stillness of the twilight hours seemed to magnify the wisdom in the air.

"Swami," Leo began, his voice laced with a mixture of curiosity and uncertainty, "I understand that discrimination helps with mind control, but how can one truly practice it? What does it mean to discriminate between the eternal and the non-eternal?"

The Swami smiled, a soft, knowing expression on his face. "Leo, *viveka* is the practice of distinguishing between that which is permanent—eternal truths, values, and your higher self—and that which is temporary, fleeting, and bound to change. Most of the distractions we face in life are rooted in the non-eternal. These are the desires, fears, and attachments that arise from our identification with the body, the mind, and the material world."

Leo thought about his own life—his relentless pursuit of wealth, status, and external validation. These were the things that had filled his days, but now he could see how empty they had left him. They were non-eternal, like a storm that passed quickly, leaving little trace behind. The eternal, however, was something much more elusive, yet infinitely more fulfilling. It was the deep peace within, the connection to something greater than himself.

"Think of *viveka* as a scale of justice," the Swami continued, "weighing what is beneficial versus what is harmful. When you discriminate between the eternal and the non-eternal, you gain clarity about what truly serves your higher purpose and what only brings temporary satisfaction or pain."

Leo closed his eyes, letting the imagery of the scale settle in his mind. He could picture it clearly—on one side, the heavy, solid weight of truth, of spiritual connection, of lasting peace. On the other side, the lighter, shifting weight of worldly distractions, material gain, and fleeting pleasures. The scale was tipped toward the latter for much of his life, but now, through *viveka*, Leo could sense that he was beginning to shift the balance.

"Every time you make a choice," the Swami said, as if reading Leo's thoughts, "ask yourself: Is this choice rooted in something eternal, something that aligns with your true nature, or is it rooted in the temporary, the fleeting? Will it bring you peace, or will it only bring momentary satisfaction, leaving you yearning for more?"

Leo reflected on the many decisions he had made throughout his life. So many had been motivated by the desire for recognition, the need to prove himself, or the pursuit of pleasure. But now, with *viveka* as his guide, he could see how these choices had kept him locked in a cycle of craving and dissatisfaction. He realized that each of those choices had been weighed more heavily by the non-eternal, and as a result, his peace had been constantly disrupted.

The Swami's words were like a light shining into the darkness of his mind. *Viveka* wasn't just about intellectual discernment; it was a practice of mindfulness, of applying this clarity in every moment. It was a tool to sift through the noise of the world and find the stillness within.

"The practice of discrimination," the Swami explained further, "requires constant awareness. It's not something you can apply only in moments of contemplation or when you're on the mat. It needs to be integrated into your daily life. In every decision you make, in every interaction, ask yourself: Is this serving my higher self, or is it serving my lower impulses? Is it temporary, or does it lead to something lasting?"

Leo nodded slowly, understanding now that *viveka* wasn't a one-time insight—it was a lifelong practice, one that would help him navigate the complexities of the world with greater wisdom and clarity.

"Just as a scale balance opposing forces," the Swami concluded, "so too does *viveka* balance the desires of the mind with the needs of the soul. It helps you weigh your choices with wisdom, bringing harmony to your life. By constantly practicing discrimination, you learn to focus your mind on what is truly important."

As Leo absorbed these teachings, he began to see the practice of discrimination not as a distant ideal, but as a practical tool for his everyday life. It was something he could begin to apply right away, in each moment of decision, in each thought that arose. By asking himself what was truly eternal—what was truly aligned with peace, love, and wisdom—he could begin to slowly untangle himself from the web of distractions that had once consumed him.

Leo looked out across the courtyard, the colors of the evening sky reflecting his inner shift. He felt as though a great weight had been lifted from his shoulders. It wasn't just that he now understood the nature of *viveka*—he was beginning to embody it. And as he did, he knew that the scale of his life was slowly tipping in favor of the eternal.

With a quiet smile, the Swami stood, signaling the end of their conversation. "Remember, Leo," he said, his voice calm but filled with quiet strength, "the more you practice *viveka*, the more you will see the world clearly, and the more you will be able to guide your mind with wisdom. This is the way to true peace."

As the Swami walked away, Leo remained seated, the weight of the lesson settling within him. He understood now that the path to mind control, and ultimately to inner peace, was not just about mastering his thoughts—it was about learning to see clearly, to discriminate between what was fleeting and what was eternal. And with each practice, each moment of discernment, he was moving closer to that clarity, that peace, and that true understanding of himself.

CHAPTER TWENTY-FOUR

The first light of dawn filtered through the trees as Leo stood outside the meditation hall, his mind restless despite the quiet of the early morning. He had spent weeks at the ashram now, absorbing the Swami's teachings, but there was one lesson that still felt elusive—how to train his mind to behave, to quiet its endless distractions and whims.

Swami Ananda had been talking to him for days about the importance of discipline in mind training. "The mind is like a wild animal," he had said one evening, "it runs here and there, reacting to every stimulus. But like any animal, it can be trained. Through patience, consistency, and effort, the mind can become a loyal servant instead of a rebellious master."

Leo had struggled with this idea. He knew the mind could be unruly, but the notion that it could be trained felt both foreign and yet strangely comforting. It reminded him of something simpler, something he could control: habits.

The Swami approached him now, his face serene as always. "Leo," he said, "today we will speak of training the mind, much like training any other habit. The mind is not inherently good or bad; it is simply what we allow it to be. Through consistent effort, we can cultivate positive thoughts, behaviors, and patterns, and train the mind to behave in a way that serves our higher purpose."

Leo listened intently, his mind already starting to connect the dots. *Training the mind*—it wasn't about forcing control over it in a moment of weakness or distress, but about instilling new habits, a consistent practice of positive reinforcement.

"Think of your mind," the Swami continued, "like a dog. A dog is not born obedient. It must be trained through repetition and positive reinforcement. At first, it may resist, running off in every direction. But with patience and persistence, you can teach it to behave, to follow commands, to sit, stay, and heel when you need it to."

Leo could picture it: a dog, wild and untamed, running about, barking at every distraction. It was exactly how his mind felt most of the time—scattered, restless, chasing after every thought, every temptation. But just like a dog, his mind too could learn to behave, to focus on what was important, to sit still when commanded.

"The mind," the Swami said, "responds to training in much the same way. At first, you will encounter resistance. The mind will wander, it will chase after distractions, it will bark and pull in every direction. But with consistent effort, you can teach it to focus, to sit still, to remain present. The key is positive reinforcement—rewarding the mind when it behaves as you wish."

Leo nodded slowly, the analogy beginning to make sense. His old habits of indulgence and distraction had been the result of an undisciplined mind. The constant craving for new challenges, the restless need to prove himself—it was all part of the mind's desire to chase after fleeting rewards, much like a dog chasing after every passing squirrel.

"And how do I train the mind, Swami?" Leo asked, his voice tinged with both curiosity and a hint of impatience.

"What is the first step?"

"Begin with awareness," the Swami replied gently. "Just as you would observe a dog's behavior, you must first become aware of the habits and patterns of your mind. Recognize when it is restless, when it is distracted, when it is chasing after something it doesn't need. Once you are aware, you can begin to redirect it, gently, patiently, with kindness and compassion."

Leo thought about this for a moment. He had always been hard on himself, berating himself when his mind wandered or when he failed to meditate properly. But now, the Swami's words made him realize that it wasn't about being perfect right away—it was about consistency, about gently guiding his mind back when it strayed.

"After awareness comes discipline," the Swami continued. "You must create new habits in the mind—just as you would teach a dog new trick. Every time the mind focuses, reward it. Every time it sits still in meditation, reward it. This will strengthen the behavior and help it become ingrained."

Leo began to see the connection more clearly. Just as a dog learned to obey commands through positive reinforcement, so too could his mind learn to focus, to remain still, to stay present. The key was consistent practice and patience.

"The rewards," the Swami added, "can be small at first—inner peace, a moment of stillness, the satisfaction of returning to the present. These rewards will train the mind to seek stillness, to avoid distractions, to behave in a way that leads to peace and clarity."

Leo was beginning to understand the power of this process. It wasn't about forcefully controlling the mind; it was about creating an environment in which the mind naturally learned to behave, to align with his true purpose. Through consistent effort and positive reinforcement, he could train his mind just as he would train a dog.

"You must also remember, Leo," the Swami said, "that this process takes time. Just as a dog does not learn to obey overnight, your mind will not be fully trained in a single day. But with consistent practice, you will see progress. It will become easier, more natural, until the mind begins to act in harmony with your higher self."

Leo stood there, feeling a sense of calm wash over him. For the first time, he felt hopeful about the possibility of mastering his mind. It wasn't about controlling every thought with brute force, but about guiding it, teaching it, training it to align with the path he had set out on.

As the sun set, casting a warm glow over the ashram, Leo felt ready. He was ready to begin training his mind, to redirect it from its distractions and train it to focus on what truly mattered. And with patience, consistency, and positive reinforcement, he knew that he could, in time, achieve the clarity and peace that he had so long sought.

In that moment, Leo Harper understood that the journey toward mind control was not a sprint, but a gradual process—a process that required the same patience, commitment, and consistency as training a dog. With each small victory, each moment of mindfulness, he was one step closer to mastering the most unruly part of himself: his mind.

CHAPTER TWENTY-FIVE

Leo sat cross-legged on the floor of the ashram's meditation hall, the stillness of the morning surrounding him like a thick blanket. The Swami had invited him to join in a new practice today: pranayama, the ancient art of breath control. Leo had heard of it before, but he had never truly understood its importance until now.

He glanced at the Swami, who stood quietly at the front of the room, his hands in a serene mudra. "Pranayama," the Swami said, his voice calm and steady, "is the practice of controlling the breath. In doing so, you calm the nervous system and stabilize the mind. The breath is the link between the body and the mind. When you control it, you begin to control the mind."

Leo's brow furrowed slightly. Breath control? He had spent his life in the chaos of boardrooms and high-stakes negotiations, where every breath seemed to be a quick, shallow gasp, a sign of his stress and impatience. How could something as simple as breathing help him control his restless mind?

The Swami noticed Leo's hesitation and smiled kindly. "Think of pranayama as the harnessing of wind energy," he said, his eyes twinkling with wisdom. "A windmill does not create wind; it simply uses the wind's power to produce energy. In the same way, pranayama harnesses the natural flow of breath to create inner peace and stability."

Leo closed his eyes, trying to imagine the concept. A windmill stood tall against the breeze, its blades turning with precision. It did not fight the wind but used it to generate power. Maybe, Leo thought, this was how pranayama worked. By learning to control the breath, he could harness its energy and use it to stabilize his mind.

"Let's begin," the Swami said, his voice gentle but firm.

Leo focused on his breath, the steady rise and fall of his chest. The Swami guided them through the first stage: inhaling deeply through the nose, holding the breath for a few seconds, and then exhaling slowly through the mouth. At first, Leo struggled to find a rhythm, his mind wandering, his body tense. Each breath felt jagged, as though he was trying to force something that should have come naturally.

But the Swami's voice was patient, guiding him back to the breath. "Focus, Leo. Each inhale fills your body with energy; each exhale releases tension. Do not force the breath. Let it come gently, like the windmill turning with the breeze."

As Leo continued to breathe, he began to notice a subtle shift. His initial resistance melted away, and the steady rhythm of his breath seemed to settle the chaos within him. For the first time in days, his mind quieted—no longer racing with thoughts of business deals, of strained relationships, of the world outside.

"Now," the Swami said, "let's add a layer. Inhalation and exhalation are the foundation, but the true power of pranayama comes when you synchronize the breath with intention."

Leo's curiosity piqued, and he followed the Swami's instructions. With each inhale, he visualized drawing in calmness and clarity. With each exhale, he imagined releasing the tension, the fears, the distractions that had once consumed him.

At first, it felt awkward—like trying to push a river upstream. His thoughts still tried to surge ahead, racing faster than his breath. But gradually, like a windmill gradually picking up speed, the flow became smoother. Leo could feel his body relaxing, the tightness in his chest slowly easing, the storm of thoughts within him beginning to settle.

"Pranayama is not just about controlling the breath," the Swami continued, "it is about training the mind to focus, to be still. When you control the breath, you calm the nervous system, and in turn, the mind follows. The mind is like a wild horse; once you learn to control the reins, it will carry you wherever you want to go."

Leo thought about this, the metaphor sinking in. The breath, like the wind, could either be a force of chaos or a source of power, depending on how it was harnessed. For years, he had let his mind run wild, chasing after every business deal, every new challenge, every fleeting pleasure. But now, with the practice of pranayama, he was learning to control the reins, to guide his mind towards stillness and clarity.

"Focus on the present moment," the Swami urged. "With every breath, you return to the here and now. With every breath, you release what no longer serves you."

Leo felt the truth in these words. His mind had been like a windstorm, scattered and uncontrolled, blowing him in every direction. But as he sat there, breathing in sync with the universe, he could feel the turbulence beginning to settle. The practice of pranayama was teaching him that just like a windmill harnessed the wind to create energy, he could harness the breath to create inner peace and control.

The session continued, each breath more controlled, more deliberate. Leo's chest felt lighter, his thoughts quieter, and for the first time in what seemed like forever, he felt a sense of inner calm. It wasn't perfect—his mind still wandered, his body still itched to move—but it was a start. The windmill was turning, slowly but steadily, harnessing the breath to create a new kind of energy: the energy of clarity.

As the practice came to an end, Leo opened his eyes, a sense of peace settling over him. The Swami was smiling at him, as though he could sense the transformation taking place within Leo.

"You see," the Swami said softly, "pranayama is not just about the breath. It is about learning to harness the energy within you. By controlling the breath, you control the mind. And when you control the mind, you control your life."

Leo stood up, feeling a sense of lightness, as though a burden had been lifted from his shoulders. He had taken the first step in mastering his mind, and for the first time in a long while, he felt hopeful about the journey ahead. The windmill was turning, and so was he—slowly, steadily, and with purpose.

CHAPTER TWENTY-SIX

The sun was setting over the ashram, casting long shadows across the simple stone courtyard. Leo sat in the center, legs crossed, his back straight, as the Swami walked toward him. There was a certain quiet energy in the air—an energy that Leo hadn't quite understood before, but now felt drawn to.

Today, the Swami had introduced Leo to a new practice: pratyahara, the art of withdrawing the senses from the external world in order to turn the focus inward. Leo had no idea what this meant in practical terms, but the Swami's calm demeanor made him trust the process.

"Leo," the Swami said, his voice gentle but firm, "pratyahara is the practice of withdrawing your senses from the distractions of the world. When the senses are not engaged with the outer world, the mind is able to focus deeply on the inner world. Only then can you begin to truly understand the nature of your thoughts."

Leo's eyes flickered in confusion. Withdraw the senses? The world around him was full of so much to engage with—his thoughts, his emotions, the people, the constant rush of information and technology. How could he withdraw from all of that?

The Swami seemed to read his thoughts. "The mind is like a turbulent river, and the senses are like the force that pushes the water. If you can withdraw the senses, the river calms, and the mind can settle into stillness."

Leo took a deep breath and tried to focus on the Swami's words. He had come to understand that all his life, he had been caught up in the external—whether it was his business, his wealth, or his social status. Always seeking validation from the outside world. How could he turn that off?

"Think of pratyahara as a turtle retreating into its shell," the Swami said, his eyes twinkling with wisdom. "When the turtle feels threatened, it pulls back into its shell for protection, shutting out the external dangers. In the same way, you can withdraw your senses from external distractions and retreat into the stillness of your own mind."

Leo closed his eyes, trying to visualize the turtle. Its slow, deliberate movements as it retreated into the safety of its shell. The idea was simple, yet profound: protection. The senses, if left unchecked, were like an open door to a storm, inviting constant distraction, anxiety, and turmoil. But by withdrawing from them, Leo could create a space of calm within himself—a sanctuary from the chaos.

"Let us begin," the Swami instructed.

Leo followed the Swami's guidance, closing his eyes and taking a slow, steady breath. He began to focus inward, blocking out the sounds of the birds outside the ashram and the rustle of leaves in the wind. His thoughts continued to wander, but with each breath, he gently guided them back to the stillness.

"The senses are constantly reaching out into the world," the Swami's voice echoed in his mind. "The eyes, the ears, the touch—they are all seeking stimulation. But true peace is found when we turn our attention inward."

Leo could feel the tension in his body, the tightness in his shoulders, the restlessness in his mind. But he continued to breathe, each exhale allowing him to draw further inward. The world outside seemed to fade, like the faint sound of waves growing quieter as they moved further away.

"Now," the Swami said, "withdraw the senses even further. Imagine that you are like the turtle, pulling into your shell. Let the world outside cease to exist for this moment. Feel the retreat, the quietness."

At first, Leo felt resistance. How could he turn off the constant barrage of thoughts and sensations? How could he stop the cravings, the desires, the overwhelming need to constantly assess, judge, and act?

But then, something shifted. As he focused on his breath, he became aware of the subtle sensations inside his body—the rhythm of his heartbeat, the gentle movement of air through his nostrils. The outside world began to feel distant, as though he were inside a bubble of silence.

It wasn't complete silence—there was still the rustling of leaves, the far-off hum of the world beyond—but Leo no longer felt as though it was encroaching on him. It was as if he had pulled back into his own shell, just like the turtle, seeking protection and peace from the relentless noise of the outside world.

After what seemed like hours, but was probably only a few minutes, the Swami's voice returned, soft and grounding: "You have done well. This is the practice of pratyahara. The more you withdraw your senses, the more your mind becomes like a calm pond, free of ripples."

Leo opened his eyes slowly, blinking against the light of the setting sun. The world around him seemed both closer and further away at the same time. It was as though the hustle and bustle of the external world no longer had the same power over him. For the first time in years, he felt unburdened, as if a veil had been lifted.

"You see, Leo," the Swami said, smiling at him, "pratyahara does not require rejection of the external world. It simply requires that we stop letting it control us. By withdrawing our senses, we can regain mastery over our attention. This is where true peace begins."

Leo sat in silence for a few moments, reflecting on the experience. He realized how much of his life had been lived in reaction to the outside world—the emails, the meetings, the expectations. But now, in this moment, he felt a shift within himself. The distractions of the world had faded, and for the first time in a long while, he felt a sense of centeredness, of control.

"Thank you," Leo said quietly. "I think I understand now. It's not about running away from the world. It's about finding the strength to face it from a place of stillness."

The Swami nodded, his eyes filled with quiet approval. "Exactly. And from that place of stillness, you will find the clarity you need to make the right decisions—not just for yourself, but for those around you."

Leo smiled, the weight of his past decisions still heavy but beginning to lighten. He had taken another step on his journey—not just towards success, but towards peace. And for the first time, he felt ready to embrace both.

CHAPTER TWENTY-SEVEN

The morning sun peeked over the horizon, casting a golden glow on the ashram's peaceful surroundings. Leo had been in India for several months now, and with each passing day, he found himself more drawn to the simplicity and depth of the Swami's teachings. Today, he was ready for his next lesson.

As he sat in front of the Swami, Leo felt a sense of anticipation, knowing that this lesson was about something very close to his heart—human relationships. Relationships had always been a source of both joy and turmoil in his life. At the core of his struggles with Claire, his wife, and even his mother, lay unresolved tensions and unmet needs. The constant chase for success had created a divide between him and those he loved, and it seemed as though every decision he made only intensified the distance between them.

But perhaps this lesson would offer him a way to heal those rifts, to bring back the harmony he had lost.

"Leo," the Swami began, his voice serene, "today we will speak of harmonious human relations. In this world, your relationships with others are as important as your relationship with yourself. A mind that is constantly disturbed by conflicts with others cannot achieve peace. True peace comes from cultivating relationships that nurture your spirit and contribute to your growth."

Leo listened intently, aware of the deep truth in the Swami's words. How often had he been distracted by the constant hum of stress and friction in his personal life? The arguments with Claire about his work, the resentment from his mother over his move to New York—all of these had created mental noise, clouding his ability to focus and think clearly.

The Swami continued, "Imagine a symphony orchestra. Every instrument has its own role, its own unique sound. But for the symphony to be beautiful, each instrument must play in harmony with the others. If one instrument plays out of tune or at the wrong time, the entire piece is disrupted. So it is with relationships. Each person brings their own unique qualities, but for the relationship to thrive, there must be harmony, understanding, and balance."

Leo closed his eyes, picturing the orchestra the Swami spoke of. The delicate sound of strings blending with the deep, resonant tones of brass. The steady rhythm of percussion syncing with the soft whispers of woodwinds. When each section played its part, the music was breathtaking—like a living, breathing entity. But when one instrument faltered, the whole symphony would stumble, and the music would lose its magic.

The Swami's words began to sink in. Harmonious relationships weren't about control or dominance; they were about understanding and cooperation. They were about being in tune with the needs and emotions of others, while also honoring your own. The tension he had felt in his relationship with Claire wasn't just about his decisions—it was about the dissonance created by his inability to listen, to empathize, to meet her needs.

"Every relationship is a dance," the Swami said. "One person leads, and the other follows. But for the dance to be graceful, both must be aware of each other's steps. The leader must not be so focused on leading that they forget the rhythm of the dance, and the follower must not resist the leader's movement. Together, they create a beautiful flow."

Leo thought of the many times he and Claire had fought. How often had he been so absorbed in his work, so focused on his own ambitions, that he had failed to notice her needs, her desires, her pain? He had taken her presence for granted, assuming she would always be there to support him. But now, as he reflected on the Swami's words, he realized that their relationship had become out of sync, like two instruments playing at different tempos.

The Swami spoke again, "The key to harmonious relationships is mutual respect, compassion, and communication. Without these qualities, even the most loving relationship can falter. And the mind, when disturbed by conflict, cannot remain peaceful."

Leo nodded. The truth in those words hit him deeply. He had always approached relationships with a transactional mindset—what could he get from them, and how could they support his success? He had never stopped to truly listen, to understand the emotional currents running beneath the surface.

"How can I bring harmony back to my relationships, Swami?" Leo asked, his voice filled with a sense of urgency. "How can I fix the damage I've done?"

The Swami smiled gently. "The first step is to open your heart. It is easy to focus on what's wrong, to criticize, to blame. But true growth in a relationship comes from understanding the other person's perspective, and from being willing to change yourself. Give up the need to control the outcome, and instead focus on creating a space where both can grow together."

Leo's heart stirred with the realization that, in his pursuit of success, he had become so focused on himself that he had stopped seeing Claire for who she truly was—her own person with her own dreams, fears, and desires. He had taken her for granted, assuming that her love for him would always remain steady, like a constant beat in a song. But relationships, like music, required care and attention to stay in tune.

The Swami continued, "And remember, Leo, true peace comes when we stop expecting others to meet all our needs. When we learn to give, to be present for others, without expecting anything in return, the relationship becomes a space for both people to flourish. The harmony you seek comes not from perfection, but from acceptance and understanding."

Leo let the Swami's words wash over him. For so long, he had sought peace and success outside himself, in his business, his wealth, and his achievements. But now, he saw that true success—true peace—was rooted in the relationships he nurtured. It was in the harmony between him and Claire, between him and his mother, and even between him and the people he worked with. When those relationships were in tune, everything else fell into place.

The Swami stood and motioned for Leo to follow him. As they walked through the gardens, Leo felt a renewed sense of clarity. The path to peace wasn't just about controlling his mind or achieving success; it was about creating harmony within himself and with those around him.

Leo took a deep breath, feeling the stillness of the moment. He knew that it would take time to heal the rifts in his relationships, but now he had the tools—the understanding—that he needed. Like an orchestra, each relationship required attention, effort, and respect to create the beautiful harmony that was his to cultivate.

"Thank you, Swami," Leo said quietly, a sense of gratitude swelling within him. "I understand now. It's not just about me. It's about creating something together."

The Swami smiled and nodded, his eyes filled with quiet wisdom. "Exactly, Leo. And that is where true peace begins."

CHAPTER TWENTY-EIGHT

Leo sat quietly in the ashram's serene courtyard, the sounds of distant chants and rustling leaves mixing with the gentle hum of his thoughts. He had learned so much during his time with Swami Ananda, but today's lesson was one that felt especially significant. As the Swami approached him with a calm smile, Leo couldn't help but wonder how he could continue to cultivate peace in his mind, even as the distractions of his past life still lingered in his thoughts.

"Leo," the Swami began, his tone soft yet firm, "today we will talk about the healthy occupation of the mind. An idle mind is a breeding ground for negativity, for unnecessary distractions. When the mind is not actively engaged in positive pursuits, it can easily be swayed by negativity, doubt, and restlessness."

Leo leaned forward, intrigued. His mind, even after months of meditation and contemplation, still felt like a battlefield of conflicting thoughts. The pressures of his past decisions, his unfinished business, and the unresolved relationships in his life were constantly lurking, ready to invade his inner peace.

The Swami continued, "Think of the mind like a garden. If you neglect it, weeds will begin to grow. But if you carefully tend to it, planting only healthy thoughts and intentions, it will flourish. The mind needs to be occupied with things that nourish it—things that promote growth and clarity. If it is left to wander aimlessly, it will be overtaken by distractions."

Leo's eyes widened. The metaphor of the mind as a garden was simple yet profound. He had always been so consumed by his ambitions, his desire to climb higher in the world of business, that he had neglected his mind's true needs. It was as if he had planted his thoughts in soil that had not been tended to, allowing harmful weeds of worry and desire to take root.

"Just as a gardener tends to their plants, nurturing them with care and patience, so must you care for your thoughts," the Swami said, as if reading Leo's mind. "Every thought is like a seed. When you allow negative, destructive thoughts to take hold, they grow into habits that shape your behavior and your life. But when you nurture positive, wholesome thoughts—thoughts that align with your higher purpose and values—you cultivate a mind that is strong, resilient, and peaceful."

Leo reflected on his past, his constant drive to achieve more, and how that pursuit had often come at the cost of his inner peace. His mind had been like a garden overrun with weeds—unfocused, distracted, and chaotic. The constant push for success had left little room for self-care, for nurturing the things that truly mattered.

"Tell me, Swami," Leo asked, his voice tinged with curiosity, "how do I begin to occupy my mind in a healthy way? How can I start planting the right seeds?"

The Swami's gaze softened as he looked at Leo. "The first step, Leo, is to redirect your mind to activities that foster growth—spiritual practices, creative pursuits, and service to others. These are the seeds that will bear fruit in your life. Engage in meditation, read uplifting texts, practice gratitude, and connect with nature. These activities will keep your mind healthy, focused, and in alignment with your higher self."

Leo felt a sense of clarity wash over him. For so long, he had been filling his mind with thoughts of competition, profit margins, and future ambitions. It had been a constant race to the top, but it had come at the expense of his well-being. Now, the Swami was suggesting a different approach—one that emphasized balance, mindfulness, and growth.

"Also, Leo," the Swami added, "remember that discipline is key. A garden requires regular attention. It is not enough to plant the seeds and walk away. You must tend to them every day—pulling out weeds, watering the plants, ensuring they receive enough sunlight. Likewise, your mind needs constant care. Regularly engage in activities that promote peace and clarity. And when distractions arise, gently steer your thoughts back to these healthy pursuits."

Leo took a deep breath, absorbing the wisdom in the Swami's words. It was as though the fog in his mind was beginning to lift, revealing a path forward—one that didn't require relentless striving, but instead, consistent nurturing of his inner world.

"You must also recognize, Leo," the Swami continued, "that balance is essential. A gardener does not overburden the plants with too much attention, nor does he neglect them. It is the same with your mind. You must find the right balance between action and rest, effort and surrender. When you occupy your mind with healthy activities, you create an inner environment where peace and joy can naturally thrive."

Leo nodded, feeling a sense of purpose beginning to take root within him. He understood now that his life was not about endless striving, but about balance and mindful engagement with the present moment. The key to a peaceful mind wasn't in escaping from the world, but in fully participating in it in a way that nourished his soul.

"Thank you, Swami," Leo said quietly, his heart full of gratitude. "I now see how essential it is to tend to my mind with care and intention. Like a gardener, I must choose my thoughts wisely and nurture them with patience."

The Swami smiled, his eyes filled with kindness. "Exactly, Leo. And remember, just as a garden flourishes with attention and care, so too will your mind. Cultivate it well, and it will provide you with the peace and clarity you seek."

As Leo walked back to his humble quarters in the ashram, the Swami's words echoed in his mind. He could already feel a shift within himself, a quiet determination to occupy his mind with healthier thoughts and pursuits. It was time to start tending to his garden of the mind, pulling out the seeds of doubt and negativity, and planting seeds of mindfulness, creativity, and peace.

With each small effort, Leo knew, his mind would begin to flourish—just like a well-tended garden, growing in beauty and strength, with the potential to yield a life of peace, purpose, and fulfillment.

CHAPTER TWENTY-NINE

Leo sat in his small room within the ashram, the early morning sunlight filtering through the window and casting a soft glow across the space. The air was thick with a sense of serenity that he had never experienced before. In the silence, his mind wandered, and he found himself reflecting on something the Swami had mentioned in passing just a few days earlier—the imagination.

"Imagination," the Swami had said with a quiet conviction, "is a powerful tool. It can shape your reality, influence your thoughts, and create the life you wish to live. But it must be used wisely. When misused, it can lead to distraction and confusion."

Leo pondered this statement deeply. For years, he had used his imagination in the pursuit of business success—visualizing deals, expanding his empire, imagining the next big step in his career. But those visions, as grand as they seemed at the time, often left him feeling empty, disconnected from his deeper desires. Now, he was beginning to see that his imagination, if harnessed with care, could lead him toward something much more profound—inner growth and self-awareness.

The Swami had explained that the imagination, much like a blank canvas, was a tool. How it was used depended on the artist holding the brush. If the mind was consumed by fleeting desires, the imagination painted chaotic and disjointed pictures. But when aligned with higher values and goals, it became an instrument for profound creativity and vision.

Today, the Swami had invited Leo to reflect on the right use of the imagination. He had been asked to spend the morning alone in the garden, to meditate on the power of his thoughts and the creative potential within him.

As Leo strolled through the peaceful gardens of the ashram, he couldn't help but visualize the landscape in his mind's eye. He saw the vibrant colors of the flowers, the ancient trees stretching their limbs toward the sky, and the clear blue waters of the nearby river. The Swami's words resonated with him: The imagination is like an artist's brush—capable of creating beauty or chaos.

Leo's own life, he realized, had been a constant act of creation—but not always in the most positive way. His imagination had been focused on success, power, and accumulation, but the more he achieved, the more he felt a sense of dissatisfaction. Now, as he walked through the garden, he began to see that the imagination, when guided with purpose and intention, could lead him to inner peace and clarity, just as it had once driven him to outward achievement.

He paused beside a small stone fountain, its gentle water cascading over moss-covered rocks. Closing his eyes, Leo began to experiment with the power of visualization—a practice he had often overlooked in the chaos of his business world. He imagined himself standing at the summit of a mountain, feeling the wind on his face, seeing the vast landscape spread out before him. As he breathed deeply, he visualized the clarity of mind he so desperately sought, the calmness that came from within, not from external success.

The more he allowed his imagination to take him on this journey, the more he began to understand the lesson: Imagination is not merely a tool for escape, but a tool for creation. It can build the life you wish to live, or it can trap you in false desires. Just like an artist with a canvas, the mind must be directed by intention, guided by higher values, and nurtured with purpose.

Suddenly, Leo saw an image in his mind—a vision of his future self. But it wasn't the millionaire CEO he had once envisioned. It was someone completely different: a man at peace, living with intention, deeply connected to his family, his community, and his own spiritual well-being. The success he had once strived for now seemed secondary to the deeper fulfillment of living with purpose and inner harmony.

As Leo opened his eyes, he felt a deep sense of gratitude. He now understood that the imagination, when used wisely, could be a tool of transformation. It could help him create a new reality, one that was more aligned with his true self.

He thought back to his previous life in New York, how he had used his imagination to visualize business empires, wealth, and power, often at the cost of his relationships and inner peace. The imprints of that ambition had clouded his mind, steering him toward a future that was no longer appealing. But now, in the quiet of the garden, he saw the potential for a new vision—one of balance, mindfulness, and compassion.

As he walked back to the ashram, Leo felt a renewed sense of clarity. He would no longer allow his imagination to be consumed by fleeting desires. Instead, he would direct it toward building a future grounded in peace, purpose, and harmony.

"Imagination," the Swami had said, "is like an artist's brush. It has the power to create beauty or chaos." Leo smiled to himself. He was ready to be the artist of his own life, to paint a canvas that reflected the truth of who he was becoming—a man of peace, purpose, and inner strength.

And as he continued his journey, he knew that each thought, each vision, would be a stroke of the brush, guiding him toward the life he was meant to live.

CHAPTER THIRTY

Leo sat cross-legged on the ground, his body still but his mind racing. The dense air of the ashram felt heavy with anticipation. Around him, the peaceful sounds of nature—the chirping of birds, the rustling of trees—seemed to fade into the background, yet his thoughts refused to quiet. He glanced over at the Swami, who was sitting with a calm demeanor, his eyes closed in deep meditation.

"How does he do it?" Leo wondered, his mind swirling with a mixture of curiosity and frustration. The Swami, with his serene presence, seemed to be in a state of perpetual peace—something Leo had never truly experienced despite his wealth, his success, and all the material comforts he had once relied on.

The Swami's teachings had become increasingly clear to Leo over the past few weeks, each lesson slowly unraveling layers of his own inner chaos. But today, as the Swami had instructed, Leo was going to take his meditation practice seriously. He was going to sit in stillness, to connect with the depths of his own mind, and to try to experience what the Swami had described as true peace.

The Swami had always said, "Meditation is the cornerstone of mind control." Leo had heard it countless times, but only now was he beginning to grasp the significance of this practice. Without meditation, he realized, the mind would continue to be like a turbulent ocean—chaotic and unpredictable. It was only in the stillness that he could learn to anchor himself and connect with his true nature.

Taking a deep breath, Leo closed his eyes and began to focus on his breathing, inhaling deeply through his nose, holding it for a moment, and then slowly exhaling. He felt his chest rise and fall in rhythm, but his thoughts, as usual, seemed to be rushing through his mind like an untamed river.

"This is harder than it looks," Leo thought, frustration creeping in. His mind was flooded with thoughts about the business, his family, the deal he had left behind, and the future that awaited him back in New York. It was as though his mind was a battlefield, each thought pulling him in a different direction.

But then, he remembered the Swami's words: "Meditation is like a calm ocean. It may appear still on the surface, but underneath, it has depth. The more you practice, the more you access this depth."

Leo tried to picture his mind as an ocean, the surface agitated by waves of thoughts, but beneath the surface, there was a profound stillness. He let his breath deepen, imagining the waves calming, one by one. Slowly, his thoughts began to quiet. The flood of worries that had once consumed him started to recede, and in its place, there was a growing sense of peace.

For the first time in a long while, Leo experienced what he could only describe as stillness—a quiet that seemed to radiate from within, enveloping him like a soft blanket. It wasn't the absence of thoughts, but a new awareness of them—a detachment from the constant stream of distractions. Leo realized that meditation was not about forcing the mind to be still but about learning to observe the thoughts without getting swept away by them.

It was like the ocean: the waves of thoughts would come and go, but beneath the surface, the water was deep and undisturbed. The practice of meditation, Leo now understood, was not about eliminating the mind's natural restlessness but about learning to return to the calm, to the depth that lay beneath.

As the hours passed, Leo sat in silence, his body tired but his mind slowly settling into a rhythm. He felt a sense of clarity, an awareness that went beyond the surface level of his thoughts. It was as though his consciousness had expanded, stretching beyond the confines of his body, beyond the noise of his life.

The Swami's teachings echoed in his mind: "Meditation fosters peace, awareness, and discipline. It is the foundation upon which all mind control rests." Leo realized that this practice was not just a method of relaxation; it was the key to mastering his mind, to cultivating the inner strength he needed to face the challenges ahead.

He was no longer fighting his thoughts or attempting to force them into submission. Instead, he was embracing them, learning to ride the waves of his mind with grace and acceptance. Like the ocean, the mind had its ebbs and flows, its moments of calm and turbulence. But through meditation, he could find the stillness within—the center that remained untouched by the storms of life.

When Leo opened his eyes, he felt different. The chaotic swirl of his thoughts had slowed, and his body, once tense, felt relaxed and at ease. For the first time, he had tasted what the Swami had promised—the deep, unshakable peace that came from within. He smiled to himself, a sense of gratitude filling his heart.

Meditation, Leo now understood, was not just an exercise or a temporary escape—it was the path to true freedom. By cultivating peace within, he could confront any external challenge with clarity and calm. It was the key to mastering his mind and, in turn, mastering his life.

As he stood up, stretching his legs, Leo felt a renewed sense of purpose. He was ready to continue his journey—both inward and outward. Meditation had given him the tool to connect with the deeper truths of his existence, and now, he knew, he could face whatever came next with a steady mind and an open heart.

And so, like a calm ocean that reflected the skies above, Leo's mind was beginning to reflect the peace he had long sought. The journey had only just begun, but he now understood that with each meditation, he was one step closer to the clarity and wisdom he had been searching for all along.

CHAPTER THIRTY-ONE

The morning air was crisp, and Leo stood at the edge of a small courtyard, staring at the rain pouring down in thick sheets. The weather had turned suddenly, just as his thoughts had, and now, the storm outside seemed to mirror the turmoil within.

He had been at the ashram for several months, absorbing lesson after lesson, but today, as he stood alone in the rain, Leo couldn't shake the heavy weight that had settled over him. He had worked so hard to quiet his mind, to understand its workings, to master it. But every now and then, despair crept in. It was as if the progress he had made was being overshadowed by an overwhelming sense of defeat.

"Will I ever be free of these negative thoughts?" Leo thought, his mind clouded with doubt. It felt as if each step forward only revealed an even deeper layer of frustration. The peaceful moments he had cultivated through meditation felt fleeting, constantly threatened by waves of negativity. And today, the storm inside him felt unbearable.

As Leo stood there, lost in his own emotions, the Swami appeared, walking slowly toward him with his calm presence. He didn't say anything at first, simply standing beside Leo, gazing at the rain.

Leo felt the familiar frustration bubbling inside him. "I thought I understood," he said, his voice tight. "I thought I was getting better at controlling my mind, at finding peace. But this... this feeling of despair... it just keeps coming back. It's like an endless storm that I can't escape."

The Swami turned to him, his eyes filled with understanding. "Leo, despair is like the rain that comes without warning. But just as you protect yourself from the rain with an umbrella, so too can you guard against the storms of your mind."

Leo's brow furrowed. "Guard against them? How? It's hard enough to simply stay focused without these negative thoughts dragging me down."

The Swami nodded gently. "Despondency is one of the greatest obstacles on the path of mind control. It comes in many forms—doubt, fear, self-pity, or simply the overwhelming sense of futility. These are the storms that can cloud your progress. But just as you wouldn't stand in the rain without protection, don't stand idly by when negativity begins to pour into your mind."

Leo watched the rain falling in torrents, his thoughts spiraling. "But how do I protect myself? The negativity just feels so real, so all-encompassing."

The Swami smiled softly. "The umbrella is not a physical one, Leo. It is the practice of awareness and detachment. When the storm of negativity arises, you must first recognize it for what it is: a temporary disturbance, a passing cloud. It is not you. It is not your true nature. You must not identify with it. See it as a fleeting emotion, like the rain, and understand that it will pass."

Leo took a deep breath. He had been so caught up in the emotional storm that he had forgotten one of the most important lessons he had learned so far: the power of awareness. He could be aware of his feelings without being controlled by them. Just as the rain could not last forever, neither could the despair that clouded his mind.

"Like an umbrella," the Swami continued, "you must protect yourself from the heavy downpour by staying grounded in your awareness, by remembering that your true self is not defined by the passing emotions. The storm may come, but you are not the rain. You are the witness."

Leo's mind cleared slightly as he absorbed these words. "So, I shouldn't try to push the negativity away? I should just observe it?"

"Exactly," the Swami affirmed. "When you push away negativity, you resist it. Resistance only strengthens it. Instead, embrace it with awareness. Let it be, knowing it will pass, and that in time, the sun will shine again. Despondency is only an obstacle if you let it consume you. If you let it, it will continue to rain. But if you simply observe it, like a cloud passing by, you free yourself from its grasp."

Leo stood in silence, the weight of the Swami's words sinking in. The rain began to ease, the storm slowly dissipating into a soft drizzle. He could almost feel the heaviness lifting from his chest, as if he had put up an inner umbrella that shielded him from the emotional downpour.

He smiled slightly, a sense of lightness returning to his being. "I see. So, the storm will come and go, and it's not something I need to fight. I just need to ride it out with awareness."

"Yes," the Swami said, his voice calm and steady. "Just as the rain is not personal, neither are your negative emotions. They are natural, but they are not you. The more you practice guarding against despondency, the more you will find your true peace beneath the storms."

Leo felt a deep sense of relief. The storm, both outside and within, had passed. He didn't need to chase the perfect, untroubled state of mind anymore. He simply needed to be present, aware, and unaffected by the inevitable ebbs and flows of his thoughts and emotions.

As he turned to follow the Swami back to the ashram, Leo felt lighter. The rain had stopped, the clouds parted, and for the first time, he felt truly equipped to face whatever mental storms might come his way.

The umbrella of awareness was now his to carry. And with it, Leo understood that guarding against despondency was not about avoiding emotions, but about learning to stand firm in the face of them.

CHAPTER THIRTY-TWO

The sun had barely set over the ashram, casting a warm golden hue on the surrounding landscape. Leo sat cross-legged in the garden, his mind calm, his body still. The lesson of the day had been clear—he was to work on mastering his thoughts, especially the negative ones. The Swami had spoken of a key principle: the need for emergency control devices.

Leo was becoming more adept at recognizing his thoughts, understanding the nature of his emotions, and letting them pass without attaching his identity to them. But there was one thing he hadn't fully mastered yet: how to respond when his emotions overwhelmed him—when anger, anxiety, or frustration surged unexpectedly.

"Can the mind be controlled even in the most intense moments?" Leo had asked earlier that day.

The Swami had nodded slowly, his gaze unwavering. "Yes, but it requires preparation. Just as you keep a fire extinguisher on hand for emergencies, you must develop techniques to quickly regain control of your mind in moments of emotional turmoil."

At that moment, Leo could feel the truth of the Swami's words. How many times had he lost control of his temper during business meetings? Or spiraled into anxiety when things didn't go according to plan? The emotional flames, whether they were anger or fear, could spread quickly, threatening to burn everything in their path.

Today, Leo had come to understand that mind control was not just about mastering long-term practices like meditation and discipline; it was also about being prepared to put out the fire of negative emotions in an instant, before they could take over.

Later that evening, after a quiet dinner with the Swami, Leo wandered outside for some fresh air. The cool breeze blew gently across the garden, rustling the leaves of the tall trees. It was then that the Swami, as if reading Leo's thoughts, approached him with a small object in his hand.

Leo looked at it curiously. It was a simple metal fire extinguisher, shiny and pristine.

"This," the Swami said with a smile, "is your first emergency control device."

Leo raised an eyebrow. "A fire extinguisher?"

The Swami nodded. "Yes. Just as you would use a fire extinguisher to put out an actual fire, you must develop tools to extinguish the emotional fires that threaten your peace."

Leo glanced at the fire extinguisher, intrigued. "How does this work in the mind?"

The Swami handed it to him. "In your mind, you must create techniques that allow you to act swiftly when anger, anxiety, or other negative emotions arise. Just as you would not stand idly by while a fire rages, you must not allow your mind to be consumed by emotion. You must have tools ready, and you must know how to use them."

Leo held the fire extinguisher in his hands, feeling its weight. "So, what exactly am I supposed to do when I feel anger or anxiety coming on?"

The Swami smiled gently. "First, recognize the emotion as soon as it arises. Awareness is the first step. When you feel the spark of anger, the twist of anxiety in your chest, you must act quickly. The fire extinguisher is not for the long-term. It's a tool for immediate relief."

Leo nodded, trying to absorb the lesson. The Swami continued, "In such moments, you can use a technique like focused breathing to calm your nervous system. The act of focusing on your breath, feeling the air flow in and out, is like the first burst of the fire extinguisher. It doesn't put out the fire completely, but it prevents it from spreading. You can also use affirmations or mantras, simple statements of truth that help reframe your emotional state. By doing this, you release the initial pressure of emotion before it escalates."

The Swami's words made sense, but Leo still felt a lingering doubt. Could these techniques really work when the emotions were so intense?

"To test it," the Swami continued, as if sensing Leo's uncertainty, "I want you to go into the city tomorrow. Spend time in a busy marketplace. Let the chaos of the crowds, the noise, and the pace of life push you to your limits. Then, when you feel yourself becoming overwhelmed, use your emergency controls. See how quickly you can regain your peace."

Leo hesitated, his mind already imagining the rush of emotions he might face. But then, a sense of determination surfaced. If he could learn to control his mind in such a volatile environment, he would have gained something truly valuable.

The next day, Leo found himself in the heart of a bustling marketplace in the city. The noise, the smells, the constant jostling of people—it was overwhelming. He could feel his stress levels rising, his chest tightening, the beginnings of frustration building.

Then, just as the Swami had instructed, Leo took a deep breath. He felt the surge of emotion, but instead of letting it take control, he began to breathe deeply, focusing on the sensation of the air entering and leaving his body. Slowly, the intensity of his feelings began to subside. The tightening in his chest loosened, and the frustration began to fade into the background.

Leo smiled to himself. The fire extinguisher had worked.

The more he practiced, the better he became at spotting the early signs of emotional disturbance. The fire extinguisher wasn't always perfect, but it was enough to stop the emotional flames from growing into a blaze that consumed him.

Over the coming days, Leo continued to develop his emergency control techniques. He added more tools to his mental toolbox: short mantras, visualization exercises, grounding techniques. Each one served as a way to take control of his emotions before they could overtake him.

He realized that controlling his mind wasn't just about long-term discipline—it was also about acting quickly when moments of emotional turbulence arose. And with these emergency controls in place, Leo began to feel more in command of himself, more at peace in the face of life's inevitable challenges.

The fire extinguisher had been a symbol of power and control. But in the end, Leo understood that the true power lay not in the tool itself, but in his ability to use it with awareness and purpose.

The emotional fires could no longer rage unchecked. Leo had learned to put them out, one breath at a time.

CHAPTER THIRTY-THREE

The early morning light filtered through the trees, casting long shadows across the ashram's courtyard. Leo stood by the window in his small room, gazing out at the vast Himalayan mountains. The quiet peace of the place seemed worlds away from the relentless pace of his old life in New York. With each passing day, Leo felt himself transforming. The teachings of the Swami had begun to take root in his heart and mind.

This morning, the Swami had instructed Leo on the power of directed thought—the art of focusing the mind intentionally on positive ideas and goals. It was an essential practice for controlling the wandering, often chaotic nature of the mind.

Leo had been struggling with this concept at first. His mind, accustomed to constant business demands and ever-shifting priorities, was a whirlwind of thoughts, distractions, and anxieties. But the Swami had told him that directed thought was a way to train the mind, much like an archer training their aim.

"A mind without direction," the Swami had said earlier that day, "is like an arrow released without aim—it will wander aimlessly and never reach its true target. But with directed thought, you choose your aim and guide your mind toward it with purpose."

Now, as Leo stood by the window, he felt the weight of those words. The mind, he realized, could be trained. It was not a wild force beyond his control; it was a tool that, when directed properly, could bring him closer to the clarity and peace he sought.

Leo turned away from the window and walked outside. The cool mountain air greeted him as he made his way to the meditation space. The Swami was already there, sitting quietly, his posture straight and serene.

"Today," the Swami said, looking up as Leo approached, "we will practice directed thought together. I will show you how to focus your mind on a positive idea, an intention that you can carry with you throughout your day. This practice is simple, but powerful. If you can master it, you can direct your thoughts towards anything you choose, shaping your mind instead of letting it shape you."

Leo nodded, eager to understand more. He sat down across from the Swami, who motioned for him to close his eyes.

"First, breathe deeply," the Swami instructed, his voice steady. "Focus on your breath. Let your awareness settle into the present moment. With each inhalation, feel yourself becoming more centered. With each exhalation, release any tension or distractions."

Leo followed the instructions, feeling his body relax with each breath. The chatter of his mind—the nagging doubts, the thoughts of his past life—began to fade into the background. As he settled into stillness, the Swami continued.

"Now, I want you to choose a thought, a positive idea, and direct your mind toward it. Imagine it clearly, as if it were already a reality. Picture it vividly in your mind, like an archer aiming at a target. You are in control. Your thought is the arrow, and the target is your highest intention."

Leo focused, allowing his mind to fixate on a single, clear thought—inner peace. He imagined himself living a life where his mind was calm, free from the incessant noise of anxiety and stress. He visualized each moment filled with tranquility, each decision guided by clarity.

As he concentrated, he could feel his mind becoming sharper, more focused. The distractions, once so overwhelming, seemed distant, irrelevant.

"Directed thought," the Swami's voice broke through Leo's concentration, "is like aiming an arrow at a target. Your thoughts must be purposeful, clear, and unwavering. If you lose focus, if the mind starts to wander, gently guide it back, just as an archer corrects their aim if the arrow drifts. Over time, with practice, you will find that the more you focus on positive thoughts, the more natural it becomes."

Leo took in the Swami's words, feeling the weight of their simplicity and truth. He had spent so much of his life caught in the whirlwind of his own thoughts, constantly reacting to circumstances. But now, in this stillness, he understood that he could choose his thoughts, that he had the power to direct them.

After several minutes of focusing on his intention, Leo opened his eyes and looked at the Swami. The clarity in his mind was palpable. He felt lighter, more focused. It was as if the fog that had clouded his thoughts had begun to lift.

"Good," the Swami said, nodding with approval. "Remember, it is not enough to simply practice this once or twice. Directed thought is a skill that must be honed, day by day. Just as an archer practices to perfect their aim, so must you practice to perfect the direction of your thoughts."

Leo felt a surge of gratitude toward the Swami. In just a short time, he had been shown a method for transforming his mind, for redirecting his energies toward what truly mattered. No longer would he be at the mercy of his scattered thoughts. With each practice of directed thought, he would guide his mind toward peace, purpose, and clarity.

As Leo left the meditation space that morning, he carried with him a new sense of empowerment. The thoughts that had once controlled him were now at his command. They were no longer the wild, untamed arrows. He was the archer, and he would direct his mind toward the target of his highest aspirations.

With each breath, each focused thought, he was taking aim at a new reality—a reality of peace, balance, and inner strength. Just like an arrow hitting its mark, Leo's directed thoughts would shape his future, one intention at a time.

CHAPTER THIRTY-FOUR

The sun had begun to set behind the peaks of the Himalayas, casting a golden glow over the tranquil landscape. Leo sat by a quiet riverbank, the gentle sound of the flowing water calming his mind. His thoughts, which had once been a constant whirlwind of worry and ambition, now felt more like ripples in a calm lake—fleeting and easy to observe.

It had taken time, but Leo was beginning to understand the secret to mastering his thoughts. The Swami's teachings had led him to this moment—one of profound clarity and self-awareness.

That morning, the Swami had spoken to him about the control of thought and its true secret: mindfulness.

"Mindfulness," the Swami had explained, "is the art of being fully aware of your thoughts and actions in the present moment. It is about observing your mind as it works, and learning to redirect your thoughts when they stray from the path you wish to follow."

Leo, who had spent years chasing success without ever truly considering the nature of his thoughts, now found himself grappling with this new idea. His mind, so accustomed to rushing toward the next big goal, often slipped into automatic mode—thinking without awareness, reacting without pause. But the Swami had told him that true mastery over the mind came through noticing the subtle shifts in thought and gently steering them back toward a purposeful direction.

"Imagine your mind is like a magnifying glass," the Swami had said earlier that day, his voice steady and calm. "When you focus your attention on a single thought, it magnifies, intensifying its power. If you choose your thoughts with mindfulness, you can amplify their positive effects. But if you allow the mind to wander without awareness, it can magnify negative thoughts just as easily."

Leo had felt the weight of those words. He had been living his life as though his thoughts were mere background noise, allowing them to guide him without questioning their direction. But now, in the stillness of the Himalayas, he was learning to observe them, to become aware of their patterns and redirect them as needed.

Now, as Leo sat by the river, he held a small magnifying glass in his hand, a gift from the Swami. It was a simple tool, but in Leo's hands, it had become a symbol of the mindfulness he had begun to cultivate.

He focused the magnifying glass on a leaf drifting gently in the current, watching it grow larger and sharper in his field of vision. The sunlight reflected off the lens, creating a small, intense beam. Leo marveled at how such a small object could have such a powerful effect when focused properly.

"Just like this magnifying glass," he thought to himself, "my mind can either magnify the good or the bad. The key is to focus intentionally, to bring awareness to my thoughts and guide them with purpose."

As Leo sat there, reflecting on the Swami's words, he realized that controlling his thoughts was not about force or suppression. It wasn't about fighting against the natural flow of his mind, but about becoming aware of the currents within it and gently steering them in a direction that aligned with his highest intentions.

With each breath, Leo practiced the art of mindfulness. When his mind wandered to a troubling thought, he observed it without judgment, simply noticing it. Then, like the beam of light through the magnifying glass, he redirected it—focusing on positive intentions, on thoughts of peace, clarity, and purpose.

Over time, Leo found that the more he practiced mindfulness, the more natural it became to control his thoughts. The negative, self-sabotaging patterns that once governed his mind began to lose their power. Each time he caught a thought before it spiraled into anxiety or doubt, he felt a sense of accomplishment, like a sculptor shaping a piece of marble into something beautiful.

The Swami's voice echoed in his mind: *"To control thought is to control the direction of your life."*

Leo had spent years controlling his external world—his businesses, his wealth, his relationships. But it was only now, in the quietude of the ashram, that he was beginning to understand the most important lesson of all: to control the mind is to control everything.

Just as a magnifying glass concentrates light, Leo was learning to focus his mental energy on the things that mattered most—his inner peace, his clarity, and his purpose. And with each passing day, he felt the power of mindfulness growing stronger within him.

As the sun set over the mountains, Leo stood up and walked back toward the meditation hall, the magnifying glass still in his hand. He smiled to himself, feeling a deep sense of gratitude. For the first time in his life, he felt truly in control—not of the world around him, but of the one thing that truly mattered: his own mind.

CHAPTER THIRTY-FIVE

The morning air in the Himalayas was crisp, and Leo felt the weight of the mountain around him as he stepped out of his room. He had become accustomed to the stillness and serenity of the ashram, but today, there was a new energy within him—a quiet curiosity about the deeper layers of his own mind.

For the past few days, the Swami had spoken about the power of the subconscious mind. "The conscious mind is just the tip of the iceberg," the Swami had said during their morning meditation. "Beneath it lies the vast, unexplored territory of the subconscious, where our deepest beliefs, fears, and desires are stored. It is here that true transformation begins."

Leo had listened attentively but had struggled to understand. He was used to logic, to business strategies and concrete results, not the abstract nature of the mind. But the Swami had promised that if Leo could learn to control his subconscious, he would unlock untapped potential within himself—potential that would influence not only his thoughts but also his actions and experiences.

That afternoon, Leo was walking by the river when the Swami found him, as if by design. The Swami smiled gently, his eyes twinkling with wisdom.

"Are you ready for today's lesson?" the Swami asked.

Leo nodded, eager yet uncertain. "What is it?"

"The subconscious mind, Leo. It is like the depths of the ocean," the Swami said, his voice calm yet powerful. "It is vast and mysterious, full of hidden treasures. But it is also filled with murky waters—unresolved fears, limiting beliefs, and suppressed desires. If you want to dive deep, you must first learn to navigate the depths."

The Swami handed Leo a small object—a diver's mask.

"This," the Swami continued, "represents the tools you will need to explore your subconscious mind. Just as a diver wears a mask to see clearly underwater, you will need techniques to see clearly within your own mind."

Leo took the mask in his hands, his mind racing with thoughts of what the Swami meant. He had no idea how the subconscious mind worked or how he could change it. But he trusted the Swami. He had to.

"The first technique is auto-suggestion," the Swami said, watching Leo closely. "It is the practice of repeating positive affirmations to yourself. Just as a diver goes deeper and deeper into the ocean, you will dive deeper into your subconscious through the repetition of affirmations. With time, these affirmations will become ingrained in your subconscious, reshaping your beliefs and behaviors."

Leo felt a spark of realization. He had always been aware of the power of thoughts but had never fully understood how deeply they could influence his life. He had spent so much time focusing on the external world, on his business and wealth, that he had neglected the internal world of his mind.

The Swami spoke again, his words simple yet profound. "The subconscious mind doesn't distinguish between reality and imagination. When you repeat positive thoughts, the subconscious accepts them as truths, and your reality begins to shift accordingly."

Leo's thoughts turned inward, to the years of negative self-talk he had harbored—self-doubt, fear of failure, insecurities about his worth. He had always believed in the power of ambition and achievement, but now, he realized, his deepest beliefs had been shaped by fears and limitations.

"The second technique," the Swami continued, "is visualization. Imagine the life you want to live, the person you wish to become. The subconscious is like a fertile garden. If you plant seeds of positive images and thoughts, it will eventually yield beautiful fruits."

Leo closed his eyes and visualized himself—calm, confident, and at peace. He saw himself leading not just a successful business, but a life filled with purpose and fulfillment. He imagined feeling the love of his family, the joy of helping others, and the peace that came from mastering his mind.

He could feel the shift happening within him. It wasn't immediate, but it was there—like the first signs of dawn breaking after a long night.

"The subconscious mind is like the depths of the ocean," the Swami said, his voice gentle yet strong. "It is not something to fear. It is not something to resist. It is something to explore, to understand, and to transform."

Leo's mind drifted to the metaphor of the diver, exploring the vast, unknown depths of the sea. In the same way, he was beginning to explore the subconscious, uncovering its hidden treasures and learning how to reshape them. Just as a diver uncovers valuable gems by carefully navigating the waters, Leo was beginning to uncover the truths of his own mind, replacing the limiting beliefs with empowering ones.

The Swami handed Leo a small stone—smooth and polished, like a treasure pulled from the deep.

"This," the Swami said, "is the result of a well-explored mind. It is the clarity that comes from diving deep, from uncovering the treasures hidden beneath the surface. And just as a diver carefully navigates the waters, you must approach your subconscious mind with patience and awareness."

Leo held the stone in his hand, feeling its weight and smoothness. It symbolized the transformation he was undergoing—a process of diving into the depths of his mind, uncovering hidden treasures, and reshaping his beliefs.

As he looked out at the river, the waters now seemed clearer, more peaceful. The turbulent currents of his mind were slowly calming. Leo felt a sense of control he had never known before, not over the world outside of him, but over the world within.

And in that moment, Leo realized that the true treasure was not just the external success he had chased for so long. The true treasure was the peaceful, empowered mind that he was beginning to create—one thought, one affirmation, one visualization at a time.

The ocean of his subconscious was vast, but Leo was learning how to dive deeper, how to explore, and how to uncover the hidden gems within himself.

CHAPTER THIRTY-SIX

The sun was setting behind the towering peaks of the Himalayas, casting long shadows over the ashram. The golden light filtered through the trees, bathing the tranquil landscape in a serene glow. Leo sat by the stone bench outside his modest room, his mind restless. Despite the profound lessons he had been receiving from the Swami, he couldn't shake the feeling that something was lurking just beneath the surface of his thoughts—something that was trying to distract him, to pull him away from the truth he was beginning to understand.

It had been months since Leo's arrival in the ashram. Each day brought new insights, new revelations about the nature of the mind. Yet, there were moments—fleeting yet potent—when Leo could sense his mind resisting the process. It was subtle, like a whisper in the back of his head, telling him that the lessons weren't important or that he was simply wasting his time in the mountains. The very thing he was trying to control—his mind—was subtly trying to sabotage his efforts.

Leo had noticed this before, in moments when he tried to meditate or practice his affirmations. Just as he settled into stillness, a thought would arise, seemingly out of nowhere, telling him that he was too busy to meditate, that he would be more productive if he simply focused on his business, that there was no point in this whole journey.

It was almost as if his mind had become a magician, pulling illusions out of thin air to divert his attention from what truly mattered. But this time, Leo was prepared. He had begun to understand the trick.

As Leo sat lost in thought, the Swami appeared beside him, as if he had been waiting for this very moment. He smiled knowingly, his eyes twinkling.

"You are seeing it, aren't you?" the Swami said, his voice calm and measured. "The mind has a way of deceiving us."

Leo nodded slowly, feeling a mixture of frustration and realization. "It's like there's always something pulling me away. I feel like I'm getting close to something important, but then... distractions appear."

The Swami nodded, his expression compassionate. "This is the trick of the mind. It is a master illusionist, constantly throwing distractions in your path, creating excuses to avoid the difficult work of self-mastery."

Leo's mind wandered back to the moments when his thoughts had wandered during meditation. "It's like it doesn't want to face the truth," he murmured. "Like it's trying to protect itself."

"Exactly," the Swami said, sitting down beside him. "The mind is protective by nature. It resists change because change means breaking free from old habits, old beliefs, and old ways of thinking. It doesn't want to lose control. And so, it creates distractions, excuses, and illusions to keep you from the work you need to do."

Leo felt a growing sense of awareness, the kind that only comes with true insight. "It's like a magician pulling a rabbit out of a hat, isn't it? What seems like a real problem, a valid excuse, is just a trick to keep me from looking deeper."

The Swami smiled. "Precisely. The mind is a master of illusion. What seems like a legitimate thought or feeling is often just a trick—a diversion from the deeper truth that lies beneath. And if you are not aware of these tricks, they can lead you away from your true path."

The Swami paused, allowing the weight of his words to settle in. "But this is where mindfulness comes in. Awareness is the key to recognizing the tricks the mind plays on us. When you are mindful, you can see the illusions for what they are—nothing more than distractions designed to prevent you from facing the truth."

Leo's eyes widened. "So, the real challenge isn't just controlling the mind—it's seeing through its tricks, its excuses."

"Yes," the Swami said. "The mind will always resist control. It will tell you that you are too busy, too tired, or that you don't need to meditate today. It will convince you that you've already done enough. It will make you feel justified in seeking pleasure or avoiding discomfort. But all of these are tricks. And the only way to overcome them is through awareness—through the ability to see beyond the surface, to recognize the illusion for what it truly is."

Leo sat in silence, reflecting on the Swami's words. He had been so focused on controlling his thoughts that he had missed the subtle ways his mind had been resisting. It wasn't enough to just direct his thoughts; he needed to be constantly aware of the tricks his mind was playing on him—whether it was in the form of distractions, justifications, or self-doubt.

"The mind is a cunning magician," the Swami continued. "But once you become aware of its tricks, you will no longer be deceived. You will be able to see through the illusion and take control."

Leo took a deep breath, feeling a new sense of clarity. He had been working so hard to control his mind, but now he understood that the real work was in being vigilant, in recognizing when his mind was trying to pull him off course.

"Thank you, Swami," Leo said, his voice filled with gratitude. "I understand now. It's not just about controlling the mind; it's about seeing the mind for what it is, recognizing its tricks, and not being fooled by them."

The Swami smiled, a proud glimmer in his eyes. "You are beginning to see the truth, Leo. The mind is a powerful tool, but only when it is properly understood and guided. Now, go—be mindful, and remember: the mind will always try to lead you astray. But with awareness, you will always find your way back to the truth."

As Leo stood up, he felt a newfound strength within him. The tricks of the mind no longer seemed as intimidating. He knew they were just illusions, temporary distractions designed to keep him from the deeper work of transforming his life.

And with that awareness, Leo felt a profound sense of freedom—the freedom to take control of his mind, to see through the illusions, and to continue on his journey toward true inner peace.

CHAPTER THIRTY-SEVEN

The air in the ashram was thick with the scent of incense, a fragrant reminder of the spiritual energy that permeated the place. Leo stood by the window, gazing out at the vast stretch of mountains that surrounded the ashram. The peaks were majestic, their snow-covered surfaces gleaming in the morning light. But as he stood there, Leo felt a familiar restlessness stirring within him. Despite the tranquility of the surroundings, his mind seemed to churn with questions and doubts.

He had come so far on his journey—learning to control his thoughts, to see through the illusions of the mind—but there were still moments when he felt as though something was missing. Something that would help him find stability in the face of life's inevitable turbulence.

Leo's reflection was interrupted by the soft, soothing voice of the Swami, who had appeared silently at his side. "You seem troubled, Leo," he observed, his tone gentle but perceptive.

Leo turned to face the Swami, a slight furrow on his brow. "I've been trying to control my mind, Swami, but there are times when it feels like a struggle I can't win. No matter how hard I try, the distractions, the doubts, they keep coming."

The Swami smiled, a knowing glint in his eyes. "You are not alone in feeling this way. The mind is powerful, and it resists change. But I have a question for you, Leo. Do you believe in something greater than yourself?"

Leo hesitated, the question catching him off guard. He had never been a particularly spiritual person. His success had always been driven by logic, ambition, and self-reliance. But in the quiet of the ashram, surrounded by teachings that challenged his every belief, Leo began to wonder if there was more to life than what he had known.

"I don't know," he admitted, his voice uncertain. "I've never really thought about it. I've always relied on my own abilities, my own strength."

The Swami nodded, as if he had expected this answer. "It is understandable, Leo. Many are like you, relying solely on their own willpower. But there is something that can make the journey of mind control easier—something that can provide a sense of direction and stability even when the mind seems chaotic."

Leo looked at the Swami, intrigued. "What is it?"

"Faith," the Swami said, his voice quiet but firm. "Faith in a higher power, in a spiritual practice, or in a greater purpose. Faith acts as an anchor for the mind. It grounds you, giving you the strength to weather life's storms."

Leo frowned, still unsure. "But how does faith help with controlling the mind?"

The Swami smiled gently, his eyes filled with compassion. "When you have faith, you are not alone in your struggle. You can surrender your will to something greater than yourself. You trust that there is a purpose to the struggles you face, and that you are being guided along your path. This trust, this faith, allows you to release your need for control and surrender to the flow of life. And when you do that, the mind becomes calmer, more focused. The distractions lose their power over you."

Leo pondered the Swami's words. He thought about the times in his life when he had been most successful—when he had been fully confident, trusting in his abilities. But there had also been times when he felt lost, adrift, overwhelmed by uncertainty. Those were the times when he had relied on his strength alone, and they were often the most turbulent times of his life.

The Swami continued, his voice soft but persuasive. "Think of faith as an anchor, Leo. In the midst of life's turbulence—the waves of doubt, fear, and distraction—faith keeps you grounded. It gives you a sense of stability, a point of reference that you can return to whenever the mind begins to wander or lose its way."

Leo closed his eyes, imagining the image of an anchor. He saw a large, heavy anchor sinking deep into the ocean, keeping a ship from drifting away. No matter how violent the storm, the ship remained anchored to the ocean floor, secure and steadfast.

It was a simple but powerful image, and as he visualized it, Leo felt a wave of calm wash over him. He realized that he had been sailing through life without an anchor, relying on his own strength to keep him from drifting. But now, he saw the possibility of something greater—a sense of purpose, a deeper connection that could provide the stability he needed.

"I think I understand," Leo said, his voice more confident now. "Faith gives you something to hold onto when everything else feels uncertain. It allows you to trust that you are on the right path, even when the mind is unsettled."

The Swami nodded, pleased with Leo's insight. "Yes, Leo. Faith doesn't mean giving up your own efforts or abilities. It means recognizing that there is something beyond the self, something that can guide you through the challenges of life. And in doing so, it strengthens your resolve to control the mind, because you are not doing it alone. You are doing it in partnership with something greater."

Leo took a deep breath, feeling a sense of peace settle over him. The path ahead was still unclear, but for the first time, he felt a sense of assurance. He wasn't alone in his journey. There was a force, a guiding presence, that would help him navigate the tumultuous sea of his mind.

As the Swami turned to leave, Leo's thoughts turned inward. He didn't know if he was ready to fully embrace faith yet, but the seed had been planted. And as with all things, he knew it would take time to grow.

But for now, he had something to hold onto—something that could ground him as he continued on his journey. He could almost feel the anchor of faith, strong and steady, keeping him secure as he faced the challenges ahead.

With a newfound sense of purpose, Leo looked out at the mountains once more, ready to face whatever came next, knowing that he was no longer alone in his struggle.

CHAPTER THIRTY-EIGHT

The crisp morning air filled Leo's lungs as he stood before the Swami, the towering peaks of the Himalayas standing like silent sentinels in the distance. The ashram had become a second home to him over the past several months, a sacred place where he had shed the layers of his past self and emerged into a new understanding of the world—and himself.

Swami Ananda, now appearing even more serene and timeless than before, stood beside him, his eyes filled with quiet wisdom. It was the final day of Leo's stay in the ashram, the day he had long known would come but had tried to push from his mind. Leo had learned more than he had ever imagined he would, and now, it was time to return—to the world he had once known, a world he had outgrown in so many ways.

"Leo," the Swami said, his voice gentle yet firm, "today I will give you the final teachings that will guide you as you re-enter the world. The lessons you've learned here have prepared you, but the real test begins now. Life, in its complexity, is like the river that flows by the ashram—constantly shifting, constantly moving. But with the clarity of your mind and the strength of your spirit, you will navigate it with ease."

Leo nodded, feeling a deep sense of calm wash over him. The journey had been long, and there had been moments of doubt, of struggle, even of frustration. But here, in this quiet, sacred place, he had learned the most profound lessons of his life—lessons about the mind, about the true nature of success, and about the deeper purpose of his existence.

"The first lesson, Leo," the Swami continued, "is that the mind is a tool, not a master. In your life, you've allowed the mind to control you, driven by desires, distractions, and fears. But now, you understand that true power lies in mastering the mind. You are the master, not the servant. Your thoughts are yours to guide, to direct."

Leo felt a deep sense of gratitude for this wisdom. It was as if the Swami had taken his most fundamental misunderstanding—the belief that the mind was something external, something to be fought against—and turned it on its head. The mind was not his enemy. It was his ally. He had only to understand it, guide it, and shape it in alignment with his higher purpose.

"The second lesson," Swami Ananda said, his eyes penetrating deep into Leo's soul, "is that the mind is constantly changing, just like the weather. It is not constant or permanent. The emotions, the thoughts—they come and go like passing clouds. To hold onto them is to live in turmoil. But to see them for what they are, fleeting and impermanent, is to live in peace."

Leo took in these words, feeling their weight. His entire life had been defined by his attachment to things—his wealth, his status, his accomplishments. But now, he understood that these attachments were like clouds—transitory, temporary, and ultimately empty of meaning. He had grasped at them for stability, but they only caused turbulence in his life. To let go of his attachments, to embrace the ebb and flow of life, was to find true peace.

"The third lesson," the Swami said, his tone steady and assured, "is the importance of self-awareness. The more you know yourself—the deeper your understanding of your thoughts, your actions, and your desires—the more power you have to change. The mind will always be in flux, but through self-awareness, you will know which currents to ride and which to avoid."

Leo closed his eyes for a moment, reflecting on his journey. When he first arrived at the ashram, he was a man driven by external markers of success—wealth, power, status. He had been blind to the deeper currents that had shaped his life. But now, as he stood at the precipice of his return, he understood that true mastery lay not in controlling the external world, but in understanding the internal one. The world would continue to change, but his inner peace would be his anchor.

"The fourth and final lesson, Leo," the Swami said, "is the practice of compassion. The greatest power you can wield in this world is love. Not the love of possessions, or fame, or success, but the love of humanity, of all beings. Your success, your wisdom, your mastery of the mind—these are all tools to serve others, to uplift them, to share in the collective experience of life. Without compassion, all else is meaningless."

Leo felt a surge of emotion rise within him at the Swami's words. Compassion had always felt like an abstract idea to him—a nice concept that he had heard about in books or speeches. But now, standing here in the ashram, he realized that compassion was not just an emotion—it was a way of life, a way of being in the world. It was not something to be practiced in isolation but to be shared with others, to heal, to help, and to uplift.

The Swami placed his hand gently on Leo's shoulder, his touch grounding and reassuring. "You have learned much here, Leo. But remember, knowledge alone is not enough. It is only through practice that you will truly embody these teachings. The world you return to will be challenging, but remember that you are not the same man who left it. You are stronger, wiser, and more compassionate. The journey ahead is yours to walk, but you are ready for it."

Leo stood in silence, absorbing the weight of the Swami's words. He felt a deep sense of completion, as if everything had come full circle. The man who had once been driven by greed, ambition, and ego was no longer there. In his place stood a man who understood the true nature of the mind, the power of inner peace, and the importance of serving others.

The Swami gave him a final, knowing smile, his eyes twinkling with wisdom. "Now, Leo, go forth into the world. You carry with you the light of the mind, the wisdom of the heart, and the power of compassion. Let that light guide you."

As Leo turned to leave, he felt a profound sense of readiness—ready to face the world with new eyes, ready to step into his life with purpose and clarity. The ashram had been his crucible, the place where he had undergone a metamorphosis. But now, it was time to take the lessons he had learned and apply them to the world he had once known, to build a new life, a new future—not for himself, but for all those he could help, uplift, and inspire.

And as he stepped forward into the unknown, Leo knew that his journey was far from over. It was only just beginning.

CHAPTER THIRTY-NINE

Leo stood at the threshold of his office in New York, his hand resting on the doorframe as he gazed out at the city below. The skyline, once a symbol of his success, now felt foreign to him. The glass-and-steel towers, gleaming with ambition and power, seemed hollow, like monuments to a life he no longer wanted. Everything he had fought for, everything he had built, was now under a microscope—his new eyes, the lens of his transformation, seeing it all for what it truly was: empty.

The memories of the ashram—the quiet mornings filled with meditation, the wisdom of Swami Ananda's teachings, and the profound peace that had settled deep within him—were with him now. The calmness he had found, the clarity, was something he had never experienced before. And yet, standing here, in the heart of the city he had built his empire, Leo realized that his previous goals, the very foundation of his success, no longer resonated with him.

His phone buzzed with messages, reminders of the merger, the multi-billion-dollar deal with the tech giant that was about to change the landscape of the smartphone market. He had been the driving force behind it, pushing his team with relentless vigor, focused on one thing: growth. But now, all he could feel was an overwhelming sense of disconnection. What had once seemed like a monumental opportunity now felt like an insidious distraction. It was just another version of the same illusion he had been chasing for years: more, bigger, faster, without purpose.

In the stillness of his office, Leo felt a wave of doubt and uncertainty wash over him. But beneath that uncertainty, there was something else—something stronger. A deep knowing that he was about to make the most important decision of his life.

The boardroom was waiting. The team was assembled, ready for Leo's final decision on the merger. They were eager for the green light, for the deal that would put their company at the forefront of the tech world. But as Leo entered the room, there was a stillness in his step, a quiet confidence that contrasted with the usual energy he brought to such meetings.

He sat at the head of the table, the room falling silent. His colleagues exchanged glances, wondering what was going on. The usual Leo, the man who thrived on big decisions and high stakes, was not here today.

"Leo, we're all set to go ahead with the deal," said Jonathan, his chief financial officer, his voice hopeful, almost expectant. "It's going to revolutionize the smartphone market. You've built this vision, and we've got all the numbers to back it up. This merger is a no-brainer."

Leo looked around the room, at the faces of the people who had followed him for years, trusting his vision, believing in his leadership. They were all waiting for him to give the green light, for him to confirm their hard work, their long hours, their tireless pursuit of this moment.

But in his heart, Leo felt something shift. He no longer felt the urgency, the hunger, the drive that had once propelled him forward. It had all been based on an illusion—a belief that success, wealth, and power would bring him fulfillment. But now he knew that success, at least in the way he had defined it, was not enough. It was hollow.

Leo took a deep breath, his mind steady, his heart clear. "I can't move forward with this deal," he said, his voice calm but resolute. The words landed heavily in the room, and for a moment, there was only silence.

"Leo, what do you mean?" Jonathan asked, his voice tinged with disbelief. "This is the deal of a lifetime. This is what we've been working toward. You've spent years preparing for this moment!"

Leo met Jonathan's gaze, feeling no fear, no doubt. He had spent years chasing external success, chasing validation, and had ignored the internal world that had always been his true compass. But now, his inner world was clear, and it was guiding him.

"I understand the numbers, Jonathan," Leo continued, his voice steady. "I understand what this deal means for our business, our bottom line, and our future. But I also understand something else now. I understand that success without purpose is nothing more than a distraction. This merger, this race to the top, it no longer aligns with who I am, with who we need to be as a company."

The room was thick with confusion, the weight of his words hanging in the air. His team had been expecting a victory, a triumph to celebrate. Instead, they were faced with uncertainty.

"We've built something incredible here, something that's been about more than just numbers," Leo continued, feeling the truth of his words rise within him. "But now, it's time to redefine what success means. We need to shift our focus, our values. We need to build a company that's not just about products and profits but about sustainability, integrity, and purpose."

His eyes scanned the room, searching for understanding, for support. "The future of business isn't about mindless growth. It's about balance. It's about creating something that benefits the world, not just our shareholders. We have the power to make a difference. We need to start with ourselves, with our values, and align everything we do with that higher purpose."

Leo could see the disbelief in their eyes, the shock of a man who had once been all about the deal, the transaction, the numbers, now speaking of purpose, sustainability, and values. But beneath that disbelief, there was something else—curiosity, perhaps even a flicker of hope.

"Are you saying we walk away from the deal?" asked Jennifer, the head of marketing, her voice a mix of concern and confusion.

"No," Leo replied, shaking his head. "We're not walking away. But we are rethinking our approach. I'm rejecting the merger, but we're going to redirect our energy. We're going to build something better, something that lasts, not just in profits but in impact. Our company will be a model for change in the tech industry—a company that's as focused on the planet as it is on innovation. A company that serves the greater good, not just the bottom line."

The silence in the room was palpable, and Leo could feel the weight of their judgment, their uncertainty. But he also felt something else—relief, a sense of freedom. For the first time in a long while, he felt aligned with his true purpose.

"I know this is unexpected," Leo said, his voice calm but firm. "But I believe this is the right decision. We have the opportunity to lead in a new direction, one that will redefine success for us and for the world. I ask for your trust, your commitment to this new vision."

There was a long pause before Jonathan spoke again, his voice measured. "If this is what you believe, Leo... then we're with you. We'll support you, but we need to move quickly. The world is changing fast."

Leo nodded, a small smile forming on his lips. "We'll move at the right pace. The right pace for us."

As the meeting ended and the team filed out, Leo stood by the window, looking out over the city. His heart was calm, his mind clear. The path ahead was uncertain, but it felt more right than anything he had ever done before. He was no longer driven by the need for success at any cost. Now, he was driven by purpose—by the desire to build something meaningful, to leave a legacy not of wealth, but of impact.

The world outside his window was waiting. And Leo Harper, now transformed, was ready to meet it—on his terms, with a vision of a future that was about so much more than just profit. It was about the greater good.

CHAPTER FORTY

Leo stood in the heart of the quiet room, surrounded by the warmth of family and the peace he had fought so hard to find. The house in Philadelphia was nothing like the high-rise apartments and luxurious penthouses he had once called home. It was modest, serene, and filled with light—a place where he could breathe, where he could finally slow down.

It had been days since Leo returned to New York, rejected the smartphone deal, and shared his new vision with his colleagues. The decision had been the turning point in his life, the point where he began to move from a place of mindless ambition to one of mindful purpose. And now, after a period of deep reflection and transformation, he was returning to the place where it all began: his roots, his family, and the quiet strength of a life redefined.

As Leo sat with Claire, he felt a deep sense of gratitude for everything that had led him here. The road had not been easy, and there had been many sleepless nights, long conversations, and difficult decisions. But now, everything seemed to fall into place. The connection he had once felt was broken, fractured by his own pursuit of external success, had now been healed.

Claire sat beside him, her hand in his, their fingers intertwined. They had talked late into the night for days, peeling away the layers of hurt and misunderstanding that had accumulated over the years. She had been skeptical at first—how could Leo, the man who had been consumed by business, the one who had been emotionally absent, the one who had pushed her aside in pursuit of bigger deals—suddenly turn everything around? But she saw the change in him. The stillness in his eyes, the calmness in his voice. She felt the shift in their relationship, too. The distance that had once grown between them had begun to dissolve. He had come back to her, not just as a husband, but as a man fully present, fully engaged in the life they had built together.

Their marriage, once fragile and strained, was now a foundation of mutual respect and understanding. Claire had seen the man Leo had become—not the ambitious, driven CEO who saw the world only in terms of profit and power, but a man who had learned to master himself, to embrace the present moment, and to prioritize what truly mattered. It was through this transformation that their love began to heal.

Leo turned to her now, his voice soft, almost as if speaking a sacred truth. "You know, Claire, I used to think that success was all about what I could build, how far I could push myself, how much I could achieve. But now, I see that true success is about mastering yourself—your mind, your heart, your actions. It's about living with purpose, not just ambition."

Claire smiled, her eyes filled with warmth. "I see that now. I see the man I married again, Leo. I see the man who is present, who listens, who is ready to be here, with us."

With their marriage renewed, Leo felt a new sense of purpose. It wasn't just about healing his personal relationships. It was about using his transformation to affect real change in the world. And so, inspired by the lessons he had learned during his time in the ashram, Leo established the *Harper Foundation for Mindfulness and Inner Peace.* It was a natural next step for him—a way to channel his business acumen into projects that reflected his new values.

The foundation's mission was clear: to promote mindfulness, inner peace, and mental well-being for individuals and communities. Leo used his business skills to build partnerships with schools, healthcare organizations, and non-profits, helping them integrate mindfulness practices into their daily operations. He worked with educators to bring mindfulness into classrooms, helping students deal with stress and anxiety. He collaborated with businesses to create work environments where employees were encouraged to practice mindfulness and self-care. The foundation also provided scholarships for people from underserved communities to attend mindfulness retreats, giving them the tools to change their lives.

Leo's foundation became a hub for change, reaching thousands of people across the country. But what mattered most to him was the impact it had on his own life. The work he did for the foundation was no longer about external validation or success. It was about creating a ripple effect of inner peace, of healing, of mastery over one's own mind. It was about giving others the tools to find peace in their lives, just as he had found it in his own.

As the days passed, Leo continued to grow. He learned that true success wasn't about achievements or accolades. It wasn't about building the biggest empire or accumulating the most wealth. It was about mastering the inner world. It was about aligning thoughts, actions, and values, and living with integrity and purpose. This was the legacy he wanted to leave behind: not just a business empire, but a world transformed by mindfulness, compassion, and inner peace.

One evening, as Leo and Claire sat on the porch, watching the sunset over the horizon, Leo reflected on how far he had come. The man who had once been consumed by the need to prove himself, to conquer the world, was now a man at peace with himself. He had healed the wounds in his marriage, rebuilt the relationships that mattered most, and found a higher purpose.

"This," Leo said, as the orange and pink hues of the sunset bathed the sky, "this is what success truly is. It's not about what you achieve—it's about who you become along the way."

Claire nodded, leaning her head on his shoulder. "You've come full circle, Leo. You've learned the true meaning of life, of success. You've learned that the greatest triumph is mastering yourself, and through that, everything else falls into place."

And as they sat together, watching the sun dip below the horizon, Leo knew with certainty that he had found the path he had been searching for all along. The path to true mastery, to true success, was within. It always had been. And now, he was living it.